CW00516545

t

House
with the Mezzanine

and Other Stories

Anton Tchekoff

iBoo Press

London

The
House with the Mezzanine
and Other Stories

Anton Tchekoff

Translated by

S.S. Koteliansky
Gilbert Cannan

Volume 10

Layout & Cover © Copyright 2020 iBooPress, London

Published by
iBoo Press House

3rd Floor
86-90 Paul Street
London, EC2A4NE UK

t: +44 20 3695 0809
info@iboo.com II iBoo.com

ISBNs
978-1-64181-823-0 (h)
978-1-64181-824-7 (p)

We care about the environment. This paper used in this publication is both acid free and totally chlorine-free (TCF). It meets the minumum requirements of ANSI / NISO z39-49-1992 (r 1997)

Printed in the United States

The
House
with the Mezzanine
and Other Stories

Anton Tchekoff

The
House
with the Mezzanine
and Other Stories

Anton Tchekof

Contents

THE HOUSE WITH THE MEZZANINE

(A PAINTER'S STORY)

I

*J*T happened nigh on seven years ago, when I was living in one of the districts of the J. province, on the estate of Bielokurov, a landowner, a young man who used to get up early, dress himself in a long overcoat, drink beer in the evenings, and all the while complain to me that he could nowhere find any one in sympathy with his ideas. He lived in a little house in the orchard, and I lived in the old manor-house, in a huge pillared hall where there was no furniture except a large divan, on which I slept, and a table at which I used to play patience. Even in calm weather there was always a moaning in the chimney, and in a storm the whole house would rock and seem as though it must split, and it was quite terrifying, especially at night, when all the ten great windows were suddenly lit up by a flash of lightning.

Doomed by fate to permanent idleness, I did positively nothing. For hours together I would sit and look through the windows at the sky, the birds, the trees and read my letters over and over again, and then for hours together I would sleep. Sometimes I would go out and wander aimlessly until evening.

Once on my way home I came unexpectedly on a strange farm-house. The sun was already setting, and the lengthening shadows were thrown over the ripening corn. Two rows of closely planted tall fir-trees stood like two thick walls, forming a sombre, magnificent avenue. I climbed the fence and walked up the avenue, slipping on the fir needles which lay two inches thick on the ground. It was still, dark, and only here and there in the tops of the trees shimmered a bright gold light casting the colours of the rainbow on a spider's web. The smell of the firs was almost suffocating. Then I turned into an avenue of limes. And here too were desolation and decay; the dead leaves rustled mournfully beneath my feet, and there were lurking shadows among the trees. To the right, in an old orchard, a goldhammer sang a faint reluctant song, and he too must have been old. The lime-trees soon came to an end and I came to a white house with a terrace and a mezzanine, and suddenly a vista opened upon a farmyard with a pond and a bathing-shed, and a row of green willows, with a village beyond, and above it stood a tall, slender belfry, on which glowed a cross catching the light of the setting sun. For a moment I was possessed with a sense of enchantment, intimate, particular, as though I had seen the scene before in my childhood.

By the white-stone gate surmounted with stone lions, which led from the yard into the field, stood two girls. One of them, the elder, thin, pale, very handsome, with masses of chestnut hair and a little stubborn mouth, looked rather prim and scarcely glanced at me; the other, who was quite young—seventeen or eighteen, no more, also thin and pale, with a big mouth and big eyes, looked at me in surprise, as I passed, said something in English and looked confused, and it seemed to me that I had always known their dear faces. And I returned home feeling as though I had awoke from a pleasant dream.

Soon after that, one afternoon, when Bielokurov and I were walking near the house, suddenly there came into the yard a spring-carriage in which sat one of the two girls, the elder. She had come to ask for subscriptions to a fund for those who had suffered in a recent fire. Without looking at us, she told us very seriously how many houses had been burned down in Sianov, how many men, women, and children had been left without shelter, and what had been done by the committee of which she was a member. She gave us the list for us to write our names, put it away, and began to say good-bye.

"You have completely forgotten us, Piotr Petrovich," she said to Bielokurov, as she gave him her hand. "Come and see us, and if Mr. N. (she said my name) would like to see how the admirers of his talent live and would care to come and see us, then mother and I would be very pleased."

I bowed.

When she had gone Piotr Petrovich began to tell me about her. The girl, he said, was of a good family and her name was Lydia Volchaninov, and the estate, on which she lived with her mother and sister, was called, like the village on the other side of the pond, Sholkovka. Her father had once occupied an eminent position in Moscow and died a privy councillor. Notwithstanding their large means, the Volchaninovs always lived in the village, summer and winter, and Lydia was a teacher in the Zemstvo School at Sholkovka and earned twenty-five roubles a month. She only spent what she earned on herself and was proud of her independence.

"They are an interesting family," said Bielokurov. "We ought to go and see them. They will be very glad to see you."

One afternoon, during a holiday, we remembered the Volchaninovs and went over to Sholkovka. They were all at home. The mother, Ekaterina Pavlovna, had obviously once been handsome, but now she was stouter than her age warranted, suffered from asthma, was melancholy and absent-minded as she tried to entertain me with talk about painting. When she heard from her daughter that I might perhaps come over to Sholkovka, she hurriedly called to mind a few of my landscapes which she had seen in exhibitions in Moscow, and now she asked what I had tried to express in them. Lydia, or as she was called at home, Lyda, talked more to Bielokurov than to me. Seriously and without a smile, she asked him why he did not work for the Zemstvo and why up till now he had never been to a Zemstvo meeting.

"It is not right of you, Piotr Petrovich," she said reproachfully. "It is not right. It is a shame."

"True, Lyda, true," said her mother. "It is not right."

"All our district is in Balaguin's hands," Lyda went on, turning to me. "He is the chairman of the council and all the jobs in the district are given to his nephews and brothers-in-law, and he does exactly as he likes. We ought to fight him. The young people ought to form a strong party; but you see what our young men are like. It is a shame, Piotr Petrovich."

The younger sister, Genya, was silent during the conversation about the Zemstvo. She did not take part in serious conversations, for by the family she was not considered grown-up, and they gave her her baby-name, Missyuss, because as a child she used to call her English governess that. All the time she examined me curiously and when I looked at the photograph-album she explained: "This is my uncle.... That is my godfather," and fingered the portraits, and at the same time touched me with her shoulder in a childlike way, and I could see her small, undeveloped bosom, her thin shoulders, her long, slim waist tightly drawn in by a belt.

We played croquet and lawn-tennis, walked in the garden, had tea, and then a large supper. After the huge pillared hall, I felt out of tune in the small cosy house, where there were no oleographs on the walls and the servants were treated considerately, and everything seemed to me young and pure, through the presence of Lyda and Missyuss, and everything was decent and orderly. At supper Lyda again talked to Bielokurov about the Zemstvo, about Balaguin, about school libraries. She was a lively, sincere, serious girl, and it was interesting to listen to her, though she spoke at length and in a loud voice—perhaps because she was used to holding forth at school. On the other hand, Piotr Petrovich, who from his university days had retained the habit of reducing any conversation to a discussion, spoke tediously, slowly, and deliberately, with an obvious desire to be taken for a clever and progressive man. He gesticulated and upset the sauce with his sleeve and it made a large pool on the table-cloth, though nobody but myself seemed to notice it.

When we returned home the night was dark and still.

"I call it good breeding," said Bielokurov, with a sigh, "not so much not to upset the sauce on the table, as not to notice it when some one else has done it. Yes. An admirable intellectual family. I'm rather out of touch with nice people. Ah! terribly. And all through business, business, business!"

He went on to say what hard work being a good farmer meant. And I thought: What a stupid, lazy lout! When we talked seriously he would drag it out with his awful drawl—er, er, er—and he works just as he talks—slowly, always behindhand, never up to time; and as for his being businesslike, I don't believe it, for he often keeps letters given him to post for weeks in his pocket.

"The worst of it is," he murmured as he walked along by my side, "the worst of it is that you go working away and never get any sympathy from anybody."

II

I began to frequent the Volchaninovs' house. Usually I sat on the bottom step of the veranda. I was filled with dissatisfaction, vague discontent with my life, which had passed so quickly and uninterestingly, and I thought all the while how good it would be to tear out of my breast my heart which had grown so weary. There would be talk going on on the terrace, the rustling of dresses, the fluttering of the pages of a book. I soon got used to Lyda receiving the sick all day long, and distributing books, and I used often to go with her to the village, bareheaded, under an umbrella. And in the evening she would hold forth about the Zemstvo and schools. She was very handsome, subtle, correct, and her lips were thin and sensitive, and whenever a serious conversation started she would say to me drily:

"This won't interest you."

10

I was not sympathetic to her. She did not like me because I was a landscape-painter, and in my pictures did not paint the suffering of the masses, and I seemed to her indifferent to what she believed in. I remember once driving along the shore of the Baikal and I met a Bouryat girl, in shirt and trousers of Chinese cotton, on horseback: I asked her if she would sell me her pipe and, while we were talking, she looked with scorn at my European face and hat, and in a moment she got bored with talking to me, whooped and galloped away. And in exactly the same way Lyda despised me as a stranger. Outwardly she never showed her dislike of me, but I felt it, and, as I sat on the bottom step of the terrace, I had a certain irritation and said that treating the peasants without being a doctor meant deceiving them, and that it is easy to be a benefactor when one owns four thousand acres.

Her sister, Missyuss, had no such cares and spent her time in complete idleness, like myself. As soon as she got up in the morning she would take a book and read it on the terrace, sitting far back in a lounge chair so that her feet hardly touched the ground, or she would hide herself with her book in the lime-walk, or she would go through the gate into the field. She would read all day long, eagerly poring over the book, and only through her looking fatigued, dizzy, and pale sometimes, was it possible to guess how much her reading exhausted her. When she saw me come she would blush a little and leave her book, and, looking into my face with her big eyes, she would tell me of things that had happened, how the chimney in the servants' room had caught fire, or how the labourer had caught a large fish in the pond. On week-days she usually wore a bright-coloured blouse and a dark-blue skirt. We used to go out together and pluck cherries for jam, in the boat, and when she jumped to reach a cherry, or pulled the oars, her thin, round arms would shine through her wide sleeves. Or I would make a sketch and she would stand and watch me breathlessly.

One Sunday, at the end of June, I went over to the Volchaninovs in the morning about nine o'clock. I walked through the park, avoiding the house, looking for mushrooms, which were very plentiful that summer, and marking them so as to pick them later with Genya. A warm wind was blowing. I met Genya and her mother, both in bright Sunday dresses, going home from church, and Genya was holding her hat against the wind. They told me they were going to have tea on the terrace.

As a man without a care in the world, seeking somehow to justify his constant idleness, I have always found such festive mornings in a country house universally attractive. When the green garden, still moist with dew, shines in the sun and seems happy, and when the terrace smells of mignonette and oleander, and the young people have just returned from church and drink tea in the garden, and when they are all so gaily dressed and so merry, and when you know that all these healthy, satisfied, beautiful people will do nothing all day long, then you long for all life to be like that. So I thought then as I walked through the garden, quite prepared to drift like that without occupation or purpose, all through the day, all through the summer.

Genya carried a basket and she looked as though she knew that she would find me there. We gathered mushrooms and talked, and whenever she asked me a question she stood in front of me to see my face.

"Yesterday," she said, "a miracle happened in our village. Pelagueya, the cripple, has been ill for a whole year, and no doctors or medicines were any good, but yesterday an old woman muttered over her and she got better."

"That's nothing," I said. "One should not go to sick people and old women for miracles. Is not health a miracle? And life itself? A miracle is something incomprehensible."

"And you are not afraid of the incomprehensible?"

"No. I like to face things I do not understand and I do not submit to them. I am superior to them. Man must think himself higher than lions, tigers, stars, higher than anything in nature, even higher than that which seems incomprehensible and miraculous. Otherwise he is not a man, but a mouse which is afraid of everything."

Genya thought that I, as an artist, knew a great deal and could guess what I did not know. She wanted me to lead her into the region of the eternal and the beautiful, into the highest world, with which, as she thought, I was perfectly familiar, and she talked to me of God, of eternal life, of the miraculous. And I, who did not admit that I and my imagination would perish for ever, would reply: "Yes. Men are immortal. Yes, eternal life awaits us." And she would listen and believe me and never asked for proof.

As we approached the house she suddenly stopped and said:

"Our Lyda is a remarkable person, isn't she? I love her dearly and would gladly sacrifice my life for her at any time. But tell me"—Genya touched my sleeve with her finger—"but tell me, why do you argue with her all the time? Why are you so irritated?"

"Because she is not right."

Genya shook her head and tears came to her eyes.

"How incomprehensible!" she muttered.

At that moment Lyda came out, and she stood by the balcony with a riding-whip in her hand, and looked very fine and pretty in the sunlight as she gave some orders to a farm-hand. Bustling about and talking loudly, she tended two or three of her patients, and then with a businesslike, preoccupied look she walked through the house, opening one cupboard after another, and at last went off to the attic; it took some time to find her for dinner and she did not come until we had finished the soup. Somehow I remember all these, little details and love to dwell on them, and I remember the whole of that day vividly, though nothing particular happened. After dinner Genya read, lying in her lounge chair, and I sat on the bottom step of the terrace. We were silent. The sky was overcast and a thin fine rain began to fall. It was hot, the wind had dropped, and it seemed the day would never end. Ekaterina Pavlovna came out on to the terrace with a fan, looking very sleepy.

"O, mamma," said Genya, kissing her hand. "It is not good for you to sleep during the day."

They adored each other. When one went into the garden, the other would stand on the terrace and look at the trees and call: "Hello!" "Genya!" or "Mamma, dear, where are you?" They always prayed together and shared the same faith, and they understood each other very well, even when they were silent. And they treated other people in exactly the same way. Ekaterina Pavlovna also soon got used to me and became attached to me, and when I did not turn up for a few days she would send to inquire if I was well. And she too used to look admiringly at my sketches, and with the same frank loquacity she would tell me things that happened, and she would confide her domestic secrets to me.

She revered her elder daughter. Lyda never came to her for caresses, and only talked about serious things: she went her own way and to her mother and sister she was as sacred and enigmatic as the admiral, sitting in his cabin, to his sailors.

"Our Lyda is a remarkable person," her mother would often say; "isn't she?"

And, now, as the soft rain fell, we spoke of Lyda:

"She is a remarkable woman," said her mother, and added in a low voice like a conspirator's as she looked round, "such as she have to be looked for with a lamp in broad daylight, though you know, I am beginning to be anxious. The school, pharmacies, books—all very well, but why go to such extremes? She is twenty-three and it is time for her to think seriously about herself. If she goes on with her books and her pharmacies she won't know how life has passed.... She ought to marry."

Genya, pale with reading, and with her hair ruffled, looked up and said, as if to herself, as she glanced at her mother:

"Mamma, dear, everything depends on the will of God."

And once more she plunged into her book.

Bielokurov came over in a poddiovka, wearing an embroidered shirt. We played croquet and lawn-tennis, and when it grew dark we had a long supper, and Lyda once more spoke of her schools and Balaguin, who had got the whole district into his own hands. As I left the Volchaninovs that night I carried away an impression of a long, long idle day, with a sad consciousness that everything ends, however long it may be. Genya took me to the gate, and perhaps, because she had spent the whole day with me from the beginning to end, I felt somehow lonely without her, and the whole kindly family was dear to me: and for the first time during the whole of that summer I had a desire to work.

"Tell me why you lead such a monotonous life," I asked Bielokurov, as we went home. "My life is tedious, dull, monotonous, because I am a painter, a queer fish, and have been worried all my life with envy, discontent, disbelief in my work: I am always poor, I am a vagabond, but you are a wealthy, normal man, a landowner, a gentleman—why do you live so tamely and take so little from life? Why, for instance, haven't you fallen in love with Lyda or Genya?"

"You forget that I love another woman," answered Bielokurov.

He meant his mistress, Lyabor Ivanovna, who lived with him in the orchard house. I used to see the lady every day, very stout, podgy, pompous, like a fatted goose, walking in the garden in a Russian head-dress, always with a sunshade, and the servants used to call her to meals or tea. Three years ago she rented a part of his house for the summer, and stayed on to live with Bielokurov, apparently for ever. She was ten years older than he and managed him very strictly, so that he had to ask her permission to go out. She would often sob and make horrible noises like a man with a cold, and then I used to send and tell her that I'm if she did not stop I would go away. Then she would stop.

When we reached home, Bielokurov sat down on the divan and frowned and brooded, and I began to pace up and down the hall, feeling a sweet stirring in me, exactly like the stirring of love. I wanted to talk about the Volchaninovs.

"Lyda could only fall in love with a Zemstvo worker like herself, some one who is run off his legs with hospitals and schools," I said. "For the sake of a girl like that a man might not only become a Zemstvo worker, but might even become worn out, like the tale of the iron boots. And Missyuss? How charming Missyuss is!"

Bielokurov began to talk at length and with his drawling er-er-ers of the disease of the century—pessimism. He spoke confidently and argumentatively. Hundreds of miles of deserted, monotonous, blackened steppe could not so forcibly depress the mind as a man like that, sitting and talking and showing no signs of going away.

"The point is neither pessimism nor optimism," I said irritably, "but that ninety-nine out of a hundred have no sense."

Bielokurov took this to mean himself, was offended, and went away.

III

"The Prince is on a visit to Malozyomov and sends you his regards," said Lyda to her mother, as she came in and took off her gloves. "He told me many interesting things. He promised to bring forward in the Zemstvo Council the question of a medical station at Malozyomov, but he says there is little hope." And turning to me, she said: "Forgive me, I keep forgetting that you are not interested."

I felt irritated.

"Why not?" I asked and shrugged my shoulders. "You don't care about my opinion, but I assure you, the question greatly interests me."

"Yes?"

"In my opinion there is absolutely no need for a medical station at Malozyomov."

My irritation affected her: she gave a glance at me, half closed her eyes and said:

"What is wanted then? Landscapes?"

"Not landscapes either. Nothing is wanted there."

She finished taking off her gloves and took up a newspaper which had just come by post; a moment later, she said quietly, apparently controlling herself:

"Last week Anna died in childbirth, and if a medical man had been available she would have lived. However, I suppose landscape-painters are entitled to their opinions."

"I have a very definite opinion, I assure you," said I, and she took refuge behind the newspaper, as though she did not wish to listen. "In my opinion medical stations, schools, libraries, pharmacies, under existing conditions, only lead to slavery. The masses are caught in a vast chain: you do not cut it but only add new links to it. That is my opinion."

She looked at me and smiled mockingly, and I went on, striving to catch the thread of my ideas.

"It does not matter that Anna should die in childbirth, but it does matter that all these Annas, Mavras, Pelagueyas, from dawn to sunset should be grinding away, ill from overwork, all their lives worried about their starving sickly children; all their lives they are afraid of death and disease, and have to be looking after themselves; they fade in youth, grow old very early, and die in filth and dirt; their children as they grow up go the same way and hundreds of years slip by and millions of people live worse than animals—in constant dread of never having a crust to eat; but the horror of their position is that they have no time to think of their souls, no time to remember that they are made in the likeness of God; hunger, cold, animal fear, incessant work, like drifts of snow block all the ways to spiritual activity, to the very thing that distinguishes man from the animals, and is the only thing indeed that makes life worth living. You come to their assistance with hospitals and schools, but you do not free them from their fetters; on the contrary, you enslave them even more, since by introducing new prejudices into their lives, you increase the number of their demands, not to mention the fact that they have to pay the Zemstvo for their drugs and pamphlets, and therefore, have to work harder than ever."

"I will not argue with you," said Lyda. "I have heard all that." She put down her paper. "I will only tell you one thing, it is no good sitting with folded hands. It is true, we do not save mankind, and perhaps we do make mistakes, but we do what we can and we are right. The highest and most sacred truth for an educated being— is to help his neighbours, and we do what we can to help. You do not like it, but it is impossible to please everybody."

"True, Lyda, true," said her mother.

In Lyda's presence her courage always failed her, and as she talked she would look timidly at her, for she was afraid of saying something foolish or out of place: and she never contradicted, but would always agree: "True, Lyda, true."

"Teaching peasants to read and write, giving them little moral pamphlets and medical assistance, cannot decrease either ignorance or mortality, just as the light from your windows cannot illuminate this huge garden," I said. "You give nothing by your interference in the lives of these people. You only create new demands, and a new compulsion to work."

"Ah! My God, but we must do something!" said Lyda exasperatedly, and I could tell by her voice that she thought my opinions negligible and despised me.

"It is necessary," I said, "to free people from hard physical work. It is necessary to relieve them of their yoke, to give them breathing space, to save them from spending their whole lives in the kitchen or the byre, in the fields; they should have time to take thought of their souls, of God and to develop their spiritual capacities. Every human being's salvation lies in spiritual activity—in his continual search for truth and the meaning of life. Give them some relief from rough, animal labour, let them feel free, then you will see how ridiculous at bottom your pamphlets and pharmacies are. Once a human being is aware of his vocation, then he can only be satisfied with religion, service, art, and not with trifles like that."

"Free them from work?" Lyda gave a smile. "Is that possible?"

"Yes.... Take upon yourself a part of their work. If we all, in town and country, without exception, agreed to share the work which is being spent by mankind in the satisfaction of physical demands, then none of us would have to work more than two or three hours a day. If all of us, rich and poor, worked three hours a day the rest of our time would be free. And then to be still less dependent on our bodies, we should invent machines to do the work and we should try to reduce our demands to the minimum. We should toughen ourselves and our children should not be afraid of hunger and cold, and we should not be anxious about their health, as Anna, Maria, Pelagueya were anxious. Then supposing we did not bother about doctors and pharmacies, and did away with tobacco factories and distilleries—what a lot of free time we should have! We should give our leisure to service and the arts. Just as peasants all work together to repair the roads, so the whole community would work together to seek truth and the meaning of life, and, I am sure of it—truth would be found very soon, man would get rid of his continual, poignant, depressing fear of death and even of death itself."

"But you contradict yourself," said Lyda. "You talk about service and deny education."

"I deny the education of a man who can only use it to read the signs on the public houses and possibly a pamphlet which he is incapable of understanding—the kind of education we have had from the time of Riurik: and village life has remained exactly as it was then. Not education is wanted but freedom for the full development of spiritual capacities. Not schools are wanted but universities."

"You deny medicine too."

"Yes. It should only be used for the investigation of diseases, as natural phenomenon, not for their cure. It is no good curing diseases if you don't cure their causes. Remove the chief cause—physical labour, and there will be no diseases. I don't acknowledge the science which cures," I went on excitedly. "Science and art, when they are true, are directed not to temporary or private purposes, but to the eternal and the general—they seek the truth and the meaning of life, they seek God, the soul, and when they are harnessed to passing needs and activities, like pharmacies and libraries, then they only complicate and encumber life. We have any number of doctors, pharmacists, lawyers, and highly educated people, but we have no biologists, mathematicians, philosophers, poets. All our intellectual and spiritual energy is wasted on temporary passing needs.... Scientists, writers, painters work and work, and thanks to them the comforts of life grow greater every day, the demands of the body multiply, but we are still a long way from the truth and man still remains the most rapacious and unseemly of animals, and everything tends to make the majority of mankind degenerate and more and more lacking in vitality. Under such conditions the life of an artist has no meaning and the more talented he is, the more strange and incomprehensible his position is, since it only amounts to his working for the amusement of the predatory, disgusting animal, man, and supporting the existing state of things. And I don't want to work and will not.... Nothing is wanted, so let the world go to hell."

"Missyuss, go away," said Lyda to her sister, evidently thinking my words dangerous to so young a girl.

Genya looked sadly at her sister and mother and went out.

"People generally talk like that," said Lyda, "when they want to excuse their indifference. It is easier to deny hospitals and schools than to come and teach."

"True, Lyda, true," her mother agreed.

"You say you will not work," Lyda went on. "Apparently you set a high price on your work, but do stop arguing. We shall never agree, since I value the most imperfect library or pharmacy, of which you spoke so scornfully just now, more than all the landscapes in the world." And at once she turned to her mother and began to talk in quite a different tone: "The Prince has got very thin, and is much changed since the last time he was here. The doctors are sending him to Vichy."

She talked to her mother about the Prince to avoid talking to me. Her face was burning, and, in order to conceal her agitation, she bent over the table as if she were short-sighted and made a show of reading the newspaper. My presence was distasteful to her. I took my leave and went home.

IV

All was quiet outside: the village on the other side of the pond was already asleep, not a single light was to be seen, and on the pond there was only the faint reflection of the stars. By the gate with the stone lions stood Genya, waiting to accompany me.

"The village is asleep," I said, trying to see her face in the darkness, and I could see her dark sad eyes fixed on me. "The innkeeper and the horse-stealers are sleeping quietly, and decent people like ourselves quarrel and irritate each other."

It was a melancholy August night—melancholy because it already smelled of the autumn: the moon rose behind a purple cloud and hardly lighted the road and the dark fields of winter corn on either side. Stars fell frequently, Genya walked beside me on the road and tried not to look at the sky, to avoid seeing the falling stars, which somehow frightened her.

"I believe you are right," she said, trembling in the evening chill. "If people could give themselves to spiritual activity, they would soon burst everything."

"Certainly. We are superior beings, and if we really knew all the power of the human genius and lived only for higher purposes then we should become like gods. But this will never be. Mankind will degenerate and of their genius not a trace will be left."

When the gate was out of sight Genya stopped and hurriedly shook my hand.

"Good night," she said, trembling; her shoulders were covered only with a thin blouse and she was shivering with cold. "Come to-morrow."

I was filled with a sudden dread of being left alone with my inevitable dissatisfaction with myself and people, and I, too, tried not to see the falling stars.

"Stay with me a little longer," I said. "Please."

I loved Genya, and she must have loved me, because she used to meet me and walk with me, and because she looked at me with tender admiration. How thrillingly beautiful her pale face was, her thin nose, her arms, her slenderness, her idleness, her constant reading. And her mind? I suspected her of having an unusual intellect: I was fascinated by the breadth of her views, perhaps because she thought differently from the strong, handsome Lyda, who did not love me. Genya liked me as a painter, I had conquered her heart by my talent, and I longed passionately to paint only for her, and I dreamed of her as my little queen, who would one day possess with me the trees, the fields, the river, the dawn, all Nature, wonderful and fascinating, with whom, as with them, I have felt helpless and useless.

"Stay with me a moment longer," I called. "I implore you."

I took off my overcoat and covered her childish shoulders. Fearing that she would look queer and ugly in a man's coat, she began to laugh and threw it off, and as she did so, I embraced her and began to cover her face, her shoulders, her arms with kisses.

"Till to-morrow," she whispered timidly as though she was afraid to break the stillness of the night. She embraced me: "We have no secrets from one another. I must tell mamma and my sister.... Is it so terrible? Mamma will be pleased. Mamma loves you, but Lyda!"

She ran to the gates.

"Good-bye," she called out.

For a couple of minutes I stood and heard her running. I had no desire to go home, there was nothing there to go for. I stood for a while lost in thought, and then quietly dragged myself back, to have one more look at the house in which she lived, the dear, simple, old house, which seemed to look at me with the windows of the mezzanine for eyes, and to understand everything. I walked past the terrace, sat down on a bench by the lawn-tennis court, in the darkness under an old elm-tree, and looked at the house. In the windows of the mezzanine, where Missyuss had her room, shone a bright light, and then a faint green glow. The lamp had been covered with a shade. Shadows began to move.... I was filled with tenderness and a calm satisfaction, to think that I could let myself be carried away and fall in love, and at the same time I felt uneasy at the thought that only a few yards away in one of the rooms of the house lay Lyda who did not love me, and perhaps hated me. I sat and waited to see if Genya would come out. I listened attentively and it seemed to me they were sitting in the mezzanine.

An hour passed. The green light went out, and the shadows were no longer visible. The moon hung high above the house and lit the sleeping garden and the avenues: I could distinctly see the dahlias and roses in the flower-bed in front of the house, and all seemed to be of one colour. It was very cold. I left the garden, picked up my overcoat in the road, and walked slowly home.

Next day after dinner when I went to the Volchaninovs', the glass door was wide open. I sat down on the terrace expecting Genya to come from behind the flower-bed or from one of the avenues, or to hear her voice come from out of the rooms; then I went into the drawing-room and the dining-room. There was not a soul to be seen. From the dining-room I went down a long passage into the hall, and then back again. There were several doors in the passage and behind one of them I could hear Lyda's voice:

"To the crow somewhere ... God ..."—she spoke slowly and distinctly, and was probably dictating—" ... God sent a piece of cheese.... To the crow ... somewhere.... Who is there?" she called out suddenly as she heard my footsteps.

"It is I."

"Oh! excuse me. I can't come out just now. I am teaching Masha."

"Is Ekaterina Pavlovna in the garden?"

"No. She and my sister left to-day for my Aunt's in Penga, and in the winter they are probably going abroad." She added after a short silence: "To the crow somewhere God sent a pi-ece of cheese. Have you got that?"

I went out into the hall, and, without a thought in my head, stood and looked out at the pond and the village, and still I heard:

"A piece of cheese.... To the crow somewhere God sent a piece of cheese."

And I left the house by the way I had come the first time, only reversing the order, from the yard into the garden, past the house, then along the lime-walk. Here a boy overtook me and handed me a note: "I have told my sister everything and she insists on my parting from you," I read. "I could not hurt her by disobeying. God will give you happiness. If you knew how bitterly mamma and I have cried."

Then through the fir avenue and the rotten fence....Over the fields where the corn was ripening and the quails screamed, cows and shackled horses now were browsing. Here and there on the hills the winter corn was already showing green. A sober, work-aday mood possessed me and I was ashamed of all I had said at the Volchaninovs', and once more it became tedious to go on living. I went home, packed my things, and left that evening for Petersburg.

I never saw the Volchaninovs again. Lately on my way to the Crimea I met Bielokurov at a station. As of old he was in a pod-diovka, wearing an embroidered shirt, and when I asked after his health, he replied: "Quite well, thanks be to God." He began to talk. He had sold his estate and bought another, smaller one in the name of Lyabov Ivanovna. He told me a little about the Volchaninovs. Lyda, he said, still lived at Sholkovka and taught the children in the school; little by little she succeeded in gathering round herself a circle of sympathetic people, who formed a strong party, and at the last Zemstvo election they drove out Balaguin, who up till then had had the whole district in his hands. Of Genya Bielokurov said that she did not live at home and he did not know where she was.

I have already begun to forget about the house with the mezzanine, and only now and then, when I am working or reading, suddenly—without rhyme or reason—I remember the green light in the window, and the sound of my own footsteps as I walked through the fields that night, when I was in love, rubbing my hands to keep them warm. And even more rarely, when I am sad and lonely, I begin already to recollect and it seems to me that I, too, am being remembered and waited for, and that we shall meet....

Missyuss, where are you?

TYPHUS

*I*N a smoking-compartment of the mail-train from Petrograd to Moscow sat a young lieutenant, Klimov by name. Opposite him sat an elderly man with a clean-shaven, shipmaster's face, to all appearances a well-to-do Finn or Swede, who all through the journey smoked a pipe and talked round and round the same subject.

"Ha! you are an officer! My brother is also an officer, but he is a sailor. He is a sailor and is stationed at Kronstadt. Why are you going to Moscow?"

"I am stationed there."

"Ha! Are you married?"

"No. I live with my aunt and sister."

"My brother is also an officer, but he is married and has a wife and three children. Ha!"

The Finn looked surprised at something, smiled broadly and fatuously as he exclaimed, "Ha," and every now and then blew through the stem of his pipe. Klimov, who was feeling rather unwell, and not at all inclined to answer questions, hated him with all his heart. He thought how good it would be to snatch his gurgling pipe out of his hands and throw it under the seat and to order the Finn himself into another car.

"They are awful people, these Finns and ... Greeks," he thought. "Useless, good-for-nothing, disgusting people. They only cumber the earth. What is the good of them?"

And the thought of Finns and Greeks filled him with a kind of nausea. He tried to compare them with the French and the Italians, but the idea of those races somehow roused in him the notion of organ-grinders, naked women, and the foreign oleographs which hung over the chest of drawers in his aunt's house.

The young officer felt generally out of sorts. There seemed to be no room for his arms and legs, though he had the whole seat to himself; his mouth was dry and sticky, his head was heavy and his clouded thoughts seemed to wander at random, not only in his head, but also outside it among the seats and the people looming in the darkness. Through the turmoil in his brain, as through a dream, he heard the murmur of voices, the rattle of the wheels, the slamming of doors. Bells, whistles, conductors, the tramp of the people on the platforms came oftener than usual. The time slipped by quickly, imperceptibly, and it seemed that the train stopped every minute at a station as now and then there would come up the sound of metallic voices:

"Is the post ready?"

"Ready."

It seemed to him that the stove-neater came in too often to look at the thermometer, and that trains never stopped passing and his own train was always roaring over bridges. The noise, the whistle, the Finn, the tobacco smoke—all mixed with the ominous shifting of misty shapes, weighed on Klimov like an intolerable nightmare. In terrible anguish he lifted up his aching head, looked at the lamp whose light was encircled with shadows and misty spots; he wanted to ask for water, but his dry tongue would hardly move, and he had hardly strength enough to answer the Finn's questions. He tried to lie down more comfortably and sleep, but he could not succeed; the Finn fell asleep several times, woke up and lighted his pipe, talked to him with his "Ha!" and went to sleep again; and the lieutenant could still not find room for his legs on the seat, and all the while the ominous figures shifted before his eyes.

At Spirov he got out to have a drink of water. He saw some people sitting at a table eating hurriedly.

"How can they eat?" he thought, trying to avoid the smell of roast meat in the air and seeing the chewing mouths, for both seemed to him utterly disgusting and made him feel sick.

A handsome lady was talking to a military man in a red cap, and she showed magnificent white teeth when she smiled; her smile, her teeth, the lady herself produced in Klimov the same impression of disgust as the ham and the fried cutlets. He could not understand how the military man in the red cap could bear to sit near her and look at her healthy smiling face.

After he had drunk some water, he went back to his place. The Finn sat and smoked. His pipe gurgled and sucked like a galoche full of holes in dirty weather.

"Ha!" he said with some surprise. "What station is this?"

"I don't know," said Klimov, lying down and shutting his mouth to keep out the acrid tobacco smoke.

"When do we get to Tver."

"I don't know. I am sorry, I ... I can't talk. I am not well. I have a cold."

The Finn knocked out his pipe against the window-frame and began to talk of his brother, the sailor. Klimov paid no more attention to him and thought in agony of his soft, comfortable bed, of the bottle of cold water, of his sister Katy, who knew so well how to tuck him up and cosset him. He even smiled when there flashed across his mind his soldier-servant Pavel, taking off his heavy, close-fitting boots and putting water on the table. It seemed to him that he would only have to lie on his bed and drink some water and his nightmare would give way to a sound, healthy sleep.

"Is the post ready?" came a dull voice from a distance.

"Ready," answered a loud, bass voice almost by the very window.

It was the second or third station from Spirov.

Time passed quickly, seemed to gallop along, and there would be no end to the bells, whistles, and stops. In despair Klimov pressed his face into the corner of the cushion, held his head in his hands, and again began to think of his sister Katy and his orderly Pavel; but his sister and his orderly got mixed up with the looming figures and whirled about and disappeared. His breath, thrown back from the cushion, burned his face, and his legs ached and a draught from the window poured into his back, but, painful though it was, he refused to change his position.... A heavy, drugging torpor crept over him and chained his limbs.

When at length he raised his head, the car was quite light. The passengers were putting on their overcoats and moving about. The train stopped. Porters in white aprons and number-plates bustled about the passengers and seized their boxes. Klimov put on his greatcoat mechanically and left the train, and he felt as though it were not himself walking, but some one else, a stranger, and he felt that he was accompanied by the heat of the train, his thirst, and the ominous, lowering figures which all night long had prevented his sleeping. Mechanically he got his luggage and took a cab. The cabman charged him one rouble and twenty-five copecks for driving him to Povarska Street, but he did not haggle and submissively took his seat in the sledge. He could still grasp the difference in numbers, but money had no value to him whatever.

At home Klimov was met by his aunt and his sister Katy, a girl of eighteen. Katy had a copy-book and a pencil in her hands as she greeted him, and he remembered that she was preparing for a teacher's examination. He took no notice of their greetings and questions, but gasped from the heat, and walked aimlessly through the rooms until he reached his own, and then he fell prone on the bed. The Finn, the red cap, the lady with the white teeth, the smell of roast meat, the shifting spot in the lamp, filled his mind and he lost consciousness and did not hear the frightened voices near him.

When he came to himself he found himself in bed, undressed, and noticed the water-bottle and Pavel, but it did not make him any more comfortable nor easy. His legs and arms, as before, felt cramped, his tongue clove to his palate, and he could hear the chuckle of the Finn's pipe.... By the bed, growing out of Pavel's broad back, a stout, black-bearded doctor was bustling.

"All right, all right, my lad," he murmured. "Excellent, excellent.... Jist so, jist so...."

The doctor called Klimov "my lad." Instead of "just so," he said "jist saow," and instead of "yes," "yies."

"Yies, yies, yies," he said. "Jist saow, jist saow.... Don't be downhearted!"

The doctor's quick, careless way of speaking, his well-fed face, and the condescending tone in which he said "my lad" exasperated Klimov.

"Why do you call me 'my lad'?" he moaned. "Why this familiarity, damn it all?"

And he was frightened by the sound of his own voice. It was so dry, weak, and hollow that he could hardly recognise it.

"Excellent, excellent," murmured the doctor, not at all offended. "Yies, yies. You mustn't be cross."

And at home the time galloped away as alarmingly quickly as in the train.... The light of day in his bedroom was every now and then changed to the dim light of evening.... The doctor never seemed to leave the bedside, and his "Yies, yies, yies," could be heard at every moment. Through the room stretched an endless row of faces; Pavel, the Finn, Captain Taroshevich, Sergeant Maximenko, the red cap, the lady with the white teeth, the doctor. All of them talked, waved their hands, smoked, ate. Once in broad daylight Klimov saw his regimental priest, Father Alexander, in his stole and with the host in his hands, standing by the bedside and muttering something with such a serious expression as Klimov had never seen him wear before. The lieutenant remembered 'hat Father Alexander used to call all the Catholic officers Poles, nd wishing to make the priest laugh, he exclaimed:

'Father Taroshevich, the Poles have fled to the woods."

ıt Father Alexander, usually a gay, light-hearted man, did not 'h and looked even more serious, and made the sign of the

Anton Tchekoff

cross over Klimov. At night, one after the other, there would come
slowly creeping in and out two shadows. They were his aunt and
his sister. The shadow of his sister would kneel down and pray;
she would bow to the ikon, and her grey shadow on the wall
would bow, too, so that two shadows prayed to God. And all the
time there was a smell of roast meat and of the Finn's pipe, but
once Klimov could detect a distinct smell of incense. He nearly
vomited and cried:

"Incense! Take it away."

There was no reply. He could only hear priests chanting in an
undertone and some one running on the stairs.

When Klimov recovered from his delirium there was not a soul
in the bedroom. The morning sun flared through the window
and the drawn curtains, and a trembling beam, thin and keen as
a sword, played on the water-bottle. He could hear the rattle of
wheels—that meant there was no more snow in the streets. The
lieutenant looked at the sunbeam, at the familiar furniture and
the door, and his first inclination was to laugh. His chest and
stomach trembled with a sweet, happy, tickling laughter. From
head to foot his whole body was filled with a feeling of infinite
happiness, like that which the first man must have felt when he
stood erect and beheld the world for the first time. Klimov had a
passionate longing for people, movement, talk. His body lay motionless; he could only move his hands, but he hardly noticed it,
for his whole attention was fixed on little things. He was delighted with his breathing and with his laughter; he was delighted
with the existence of the water-bottle, the ceiling, the sunbeam,
the ribbon on the curtain. God's world, even in such a narrow
corner as his bedroom, seemed to him beautiful, varied, great.
When the doctor appeared the lieutenant thought how nice his
medicine was, how nice and sympathetic the doctor was, how
nice and interesting people were, on the whole.

"Yies, yies, yies," said the doctor. "Excellent, excellent. Now we
are well again. Jist saow. Jist saow."

The lieutenant listened and laughed gleefully. He remembered
the Finn, the lady with the white teeth, the train, and he wanted
to eat and smoke.

"Doctor," he said, "tell them to bring me a slice of rye bread and
salt, and some sardines...."

The doctor refused. Pavel did not obey his order and refused to
go for bread. The lieutenant could not bear it and began to cry like
a thwarted child.

"Ba-by," the doctor laughed. "Mamma! Hush-aby!"

27

Klimov also began to laugh, and when the doctor had gone, he fell sound asleep. He woke up with the same feeling of joy and happiness. His aunt was sitting by his bed.

"Oh, aunty!" He was very happy. "What has been the matter with me?"

"Typhus."

"I say! And now I am well, quite well! Where is Katy?"

"She is not at home. She has probably gone to see some one after her examination."

The old woman bent over her stocking as she said this; her lips began to tremble; she turned her face away and suddenly began to sob. In her grief, she forgot the doctor's orders and cried:

"Oh! Katy! Katy! Our angel is gone from us! She is gone!"

She dropped her stocking and stooped down for it, and her cap fell off her head. Klimov stared at her grey hair, could not understand, was alarmed for Katy, and asked:

"But where is she, aunty?"

The old woman, who had already forgotten Klimov and remembered only her grief, said:

"She caught typhus from you and ... and died. She was buried the day before yesterday."

This sudden appalling piece of news came home to Klimov's mind, but dreadful and shocking though it was it could not subdue the animal joy which thrilled through the convalescent lieutenant. He cried, laughed, and soon began to complain that he was given nothing to eat.

Only a week later, when, supported by Pavel, he walked in a dressing-gown to the window, and saw the grey spring sky and heard the horrible rattle of some old rails being carried by on a lorry, then his heart ached with sorrow and he began to weep and pressed his forehead against the window-frame.

"How unhappy I am!" he murmured. "My God, how unhappy I am!"

And joy gave way to his habitual weariness and a sense of his irreparable loss.

GOOSEBERRIES

FROM early morning the sky had been overcast with clouds; the day was still, cool, and wearisome, as usual on grey, dull days when the clouds hang low over the fields and it looks like rain, which never comes. Ivan Ivanich, the veterinary surgeon, and Bourkin, the schoolmaster, were tired of walking and the fields seemed endless to them. Far ahead they could just see the windmills of the village of Mirousky, to the right stretched away to disappear behind the village a line of hills, and they knew that it was the bank of the river; meadows, green willows, farmhouses; and from one of the hills there could be seen a field as endless, telegraph-posts, and the train, looking from a distance like a crawling caterpillar, and in clear weather even the town. In the calm weather when all Nature seemed gentle and melancholy, Ivan Ivanich and Bourkin were filled with love for the fields and thought how grand and beautiful the country was.

"Last time, when we stopped in Prokofyi's shed," said Bourkin, "you were going to tell me a story."

"Yes. I wanted to tell you about my brother."

Ivan Ivanich took a deep breath and lighted his pipe before beginning his story, but just then the rain began to fall. And in about five minutes it came pelting down and showed no signs of stopping. Ivan Ivanich stopped and hesitated; the dogs, wet through, stood with their tails between their legs and looked at them mournfully.

"We ought to take shelter," said Bourkin. "Let us go to Aliokhin. It is close by."

"Very well."

They took a short cut over a stubble-field and then bore to the right, until they came to the road. Soon there appeared poplars, a garden, the red roofs of granaries; the river began to glimmer and they came to a wide road with a mill and a white bathing-shed. It was Sophino, where Aliokhin lived.

The mill was working, drowning the sound of the rain, and

the dam shook. Round the carts stood wet horses, hanging their heads, and men were walking about with their heads covered with sacks. It was wet, muddy, and unpleasant, and the river looked cold and sullen. Ivan Ivanich and Bourkin felt wet and uncomfortable through and through; their feet were tired with walking in the mud, and they walked past the dam to the barn in silence as though they were angry with each other.

In one of the barns a winnowing-machine was working, sending out clouds of dust. On the threshold stood Aliokhin himself, a man of about forty, tall and stout, with long hair, more like a professor or a painter than a farmer. He was wearing a grimy white shirt and rope belt, and pants instead of trousers; and his boots were covered with mud and straw. His nose and eyes were black with dust. He recognised Ivan Ivanich and was apparently very pleased.

"Please, gentlemen," he said, "go to the house. I'll be with you in a minute."

The house was large and two-storied. Aliokhin lived downstairs in two vaulted rooms with little windows designed for the farm-hands; the farmhouse was plain, and the place smelled of rye bread and vodka, and leather. He rarely used the reception-rooms, only when guests arrived. Ivan Ivanich and Bourkin were received by a chambermaid; such a pretty young woman that both of them stopped and exchanged glances.

"You cannot imagine how glad I am to see you, gentlemen," said Aliokhin, coming after them into the hall. "I never expected you. Pelagueya," he said to the maid, "give my friends a change of clothes. And I will change, too. But I must have a bath. I haven't had one since the spring. Wouldn't you like to come to the bathing-shed? And meanwhile our things will be got ready."

Pretty Pelagueya, dainty and sweet, brought towels and soap, and Aliokhin led his guests to the bathing-shed.

"Yes," he said, "it is a long time since I had a bath. My bathing-shed is all right, as you see. My father and I put it up, but somehow I have no time to bathe."

He sat down on the step and lathered his long hair and neck, and the water round him became brown.

"Yes. I see," said Ivan Ivanich heavily, looking at his head.

"It is a long time since I bathed," said Aliokhin shyly, as he soaped himself again, and the water round him became dark blue, like ink.

Ivan Ivanich came out of the shed, plunged into the water with a splash, and swam about in the rain, flapping his arms, and sending waves back, and on the waves tossed white lilies; he swam out to the middle of the pool and dived, and in a minute came up again in another place and kept on swimming and diving, trying to reach the bottom. "Ah! how delicious!" he shouted in his glee. "How delicious!" He swam to the mill, spoke to the peasants, and came back, and in the middle of the pool he lay on his back to let the rain fall on his face. Bourkin and Aliokhin were already dressed and ready to go, but he kept on swimming and diving.

"Delicious," he said. "Too delicious!"

"You've had enough," shouted Bourkin.

They went to the house. And only when the lamp was lit in the large drawing-room up-stairs, and Bourkin and Ivan Ivanich, dressed in silk dressing-gowns and warm slippers, lounged in chairs, and Aliokhin himself, washed and brushed, in a new frock coat, paced up and down evidently delighting in the warmth and cleanliness and dry clothes and slippers, and pretty Pelagueya, noiselessly tripping over the carpet and smiling sweetly, brought in tea and jam on a tray, only then did Ivan Ivanich begin his story, and it was as though he was being listened to not only by Bourkin and Aliokhin, but also by the old and young ladies and the officer who looked down so staidly and tranquilly from the golden frames.

"We are two brothers," he began, "I, Ivan Ivanich, and Nicholai Ivanich, two years younger. I went in for study and became a veterinary surgeon, while Nicholai was at the Exchequer Court when he was nineteen. Our father, Tchimasha-Himalaysky, was a cantonist, but he died with an officer's rank and left us his title of nobility and a small estate. After his death the estate went to pay his debts. However, we spent our childhood there in the country. We were just like peasant's children, spent days and nights in the fields and the woods, minded the house, barked the lime-trees, fished, and so on.... And you know once a man has fished, or watched the thrushes hovering in flocks over the village in the bright, cool, autumn days, he can never really be a townsman, and to the day of his death he will be drawn to the country. My brother pined away in the Exchequer. Years passed and he sat in the same place, wrote out the same documents, and thought of one thing, how to get back to the country. And little by little his distress became a definite disorder, a fixed idea—to buy a small farm somewhere by the bank of a river or a lake.

"He was a good fellow and I loved him, but I never sympathised with the desire to shut oneself up on one's own farm. It is a common saying that a man needs only six feet of land. But surely a corpse wants that, not a man. And I hear that our intellectuals have a longing for the land and want to acquire farms. But it all comes down to the six feet of land. To leave town, and the struggle and the swim of life, and go and hide yourself in a farmhouse is not life—it is egoism, laziness; it is a kind of monasticism, but monasticism without action. A man needs, not six feet of land, not a farm, but the whole earth, all Nature, where in full liberty he can display all the properties and qualities of the free spirit.

"My brother Nicholai, sitting in his office, would dream of eating his own schi, with its savoury smell floating across the farm-yard; and of eating out in the open air, and of sleeping in the sun, and of sitting for hours together on a seat by the gate and gazing at the field and the forest. Books on agriculture and the hints in almanacs were his joy, his favourite spiritual food; and he liked reading newspapers, but only the advertisements of land to be sold, so many acres of arable and grass land, with a farmhouse, river, garden, mill, and mill-pond. And he would dream of garden-walls, flowers, fruits, nests, carp in the pond, don't you know, and all the rest of it. These fantasies of his used to vary according to the advertisements he found, but somehow there was always a gooseberry-bush in every one. Not a house, not a romantic spot could he imagine without its gooseberry-bush.

"'Country life has its advantages,' he used to say. 'You sit on the veranda drinking tea and your ducklings swim on the pond, and everything smells good ... and there are gooseberries.'

"He used to draw out a plan of his estate and always the same things were shown on it: (a) Farmhouse, (b) cottage, (c) vegetable garden, (d) gooseberry-bush. He used to live meagrely and never had enough to eat and drink, dressed God knows how, exactly like a beggar, and always saved and put his money into the bank. He was terribly stingy. It used to hurt me to see him, and I used to give him money to go away for a holiday, but he would put that away, too. Once a man gets a fixed idea, there's nothing to be done.

"Years passed; he was transferred to another province. He completed his fortieth year and was still reading advertisements in the papers and saving up his money. Then I heard he was married. Still with the same idea of buying a farmhouse with a gooseberry-bush, he married an elderly, ugly widow, not out of any feeling for her, but because she had money. With her he still lived stingily, kept her half-starved, and put the money into the bank in his own name. She had been the wife of a postmaster and was used to good living, but with her second husband she did not even have enough black bread; she pined away in her new life, and in three years or so gave up her soul to God. And my brother never for a moment thought himself to blame for her death. Money, like vodka, can play queer tricks with a man. Once in our town a merchant lay dying. Before his death he asked for some honey, and he ate all his notes and scrip with the honey so that nobody should get it. Once I was examining a herd of cattle at a station and a horse-jobber fell under the engine, and his foot was cut off. We carried him into the waiting-room, with the blood pouring down—a terrible business—and all the while he kept on asking anxiously for his foot; he had twenty-five roubles in his boot and did not want to lose them."

"Keep to your story," said Bourkin.

"After the death of his wife," Ivan Ivanich continued, after a long pause, "my brother began to look out for an estate. Of course you may search for five years, and even then buy a pig in a poke. Through an agent my brother Nicholai raised a mortgage and bought three hundred acres with a farmhouse, a cottage, and a park, but there was no orchard, no gooseberry-bush, no duck-pond; there was a river but the water in it was coffee-coloured because the estate lay between a brick-yard and a gelatine factory. But my brother Nicholai was not worried about that; he ordered twenty gooseberry-bushes and settled down to a country life.

"Last year I paid him a visit. I thought I'd go and see how things were with him. In his letters my brother called his estate Tchimbarshov Corner, or Himalayskoe. I arrived at Himalayskoe in the afternoon. It was hot. There were ditches, fences, hedges, rows of young fir-trees, trees everywhere, and there was no telling how to cross the yard or where to put your horse. I went to the house and was met by a red-haired dog, as fat as a pig. He tried to bark but felt too lazy. Out of the kitchen came the cook, barefooted, and also as fat as a pig, and said that the master was having his afternoon rest. I went in to my brother and found him sitting on his bed with his knees covered with a blanket; he looked old, stout, flabby; his cheeks, nose, and lips were pendulous. I half expected him to grunt like a pig.

"We embraced and shed a tear of joy and also of sadness to think that we had once been young, but were now both going grey and nearing death. He dressed and took me to see his estate.

"'Well? How are you getting on?' I asked.

"'All right, thank God. I am doing very well.'

"He was no longer the poor, tired official, but a real landowner and a person of consequence. He had got used to the place and liked it, ate a great deal, took Russian baths, was growing fat, had already gone to law with the parish and the two factories, and was much offended if the peasants did not call him 'Your Lordship.' And, like a good landowner, he looked after his soul and did good works pompously, never simply. What good works? He cured the peasants of all kinds of diseases with soda and castor-oil, and on his birthday he would have a thanksgiving service held in the middle of the village, and would treat the peasants to half a bucket of vodka, which he thought the right thing to do. Ah! Those horrible buckets of vodka. One day a greasy landowner will drag the peasants before the Zembro Court for trespass, and the next, if it's a holiday, he will give them a bucket of vodka, and they drink and shout Hooray! and lick his boots in their drunkenness. A change to good eating and idleness always fills a Russian with the most preposterous self-conceit. Nicholai Ivanich who, when he was in the Exchequer, was terrified to have an opinion of his own, now imagined that what he said was law. 'Education is necessary for the masses, but they are not fit for it.' 'Corporal punishment is generally harmful, but in certain cases it is useful and indispensable.'

"'I know the people and I know how to treat them,' he would say. 'The people love me. I have only to raise my finger and they will do as I wish.'

"And all this, mark you, was said with a kindly smile of wisdom. He was constantly saying: 'We noblemen,' or 'I, as a nobleman.' Apparently he had forgotten that our grandfather was a peasant and our father a common soldier. Even our family name, Tchimacha-Himalaysky, which is really an absurd one, seemed to him full-sounding, distinguished, and very pleasing.

"But my point does not concern him so much as myself. I want to tell you what a change took place in me in those few hours while I was in his house. In the evening, while we were having tea, the cook laid a plateful of gooseberries on the table. They had not been bought, but were his own gooseberries, plucked for the first time since the bushes were planted. Nicholai Ivanich laughed with joy and for a minute or two he looked in silence at the gooseberries with tears in his eyes. He could not speak for excitement, then put one into his mouth, glanced at me in triumph, like a child at last being given its favourite toy, and said:

"'How good they are!'

"He went on eating greedily, and saying all the while:

"'How good they are! Do try one!'

"It was hard and sour, but, as Poushkin said, the illusion which exalts us is dearer to us than ten thousand truths. I saw a happy man, one whose dearest dream had come true, who had attained his goal in life, who had got what he wanted, and was pleased with his destiny and with himself. In my idea of human life there is always some alloy of sadness, but now at the sight of a happy man I was filled with something like despair. And at night it grew on me. A bed was made up for me in the room near my brother's and I could hear him, unable to sleep, going again and again to the plate of gooseberries. I thought: 'After all, what a lot of contented, happy people there must be! What an overwhelming power that means! I look at this life and see the arrogance and the idleness of the strong, the ignorance and bestiality of the weak, the horrible poverty everywhere, overcrowding, drunkenness, hypocrisy, falsehood.... Meanwhile in all the houses, all the streets, there is peace; out of fifty thousand people who live in our town there is not one to kick against it all. Think of the people who go to the market for food: during the day they eat; at night they sleep, talk nonsense, marry, grow old, piously follow their dead to the cemetery; one never sees or hears those who suffer, and all the horror of life goes on somewhere behind the scenes. Everything is quiet, peaceful, and against it all there is only the silent protest of statistics; so many go mad, so many gallons are drunk, so many children die of starvation.... And such a state of things is obviously what we want; apparently a happy man only feels so because the unhappy bear their burden in silence, but for which happiness would be impossible. It is a general hypnosis. Every happy man should have some one with a little hammer at his door to knock and remind him that there are unhappy people, and that, however happy he may be, life will sooner or later show its claws, and some misfortune will befall him—illness, poverty, loss, and then no one will see or hear him, just as he now neither sees nor hears others. But there is no man with a hammer, and the happy go on living, just a little fluttered with the petty cares of every day, like an aspen-tree in the wind—and everything is all right.'

"That night I was able to understand how I, too, had been content and happy," Ivan Ivanich went on, getting up. "I, too, at meals or out hunting, used to lay down the law about living, and religion, and governing the masses. I, too, used to say that teaching is light, that education is necessary, but that for simple folk reading and writing is enough for the present. Freedom is a boon, I used to say, as essential as the air we breathe, but we must wait. Yes—I used to say so, but now I ask: 'Why do we wait?'" Ivan

Ivanich glanced angrily at Bourkin. "Why do we wait, I ask you? What considerations keep us fast? I am told that we cannot have everything at once, and that every idea is realised in time. But who says so? Where is the proof that it is so? You refer me to the natural order of things, to the law of cause and effect, but is there order or natural law in that I, a living, thinking creature, should stand by a ditch until it fills up, or is narrowed, when I could jump it or throw a bridge over it? Tell me, I say, why should we wait? Wait, when we have no strength to live, and yet must live and are full of the desire to live!

"I left my brother early the next morning, and from that time on I found it impossible to live in town. The peace and the quiet of it oppress me. I dare not look in at the windows, for nothing is more dreadful to see than the sight of a happy family, sitting round a table, having tea. I am an old man now and am no good for the struggle. I commenced late. I can only grieve within my soul, and fret and sulk. At night my head buzzes with the rush of my thoughts and I cannot sleep.... Ah! If I were young!"

Ivan Ivanich walked excitedly up and down the room and repeated:

"If I were young."

He suddenly walked up to Aliokhin and shook him first by one hand and then by the other.

"Pavel Konstantinich," he said in a voice of entreaty, "don't be satisfied, don't let yourself be lulled to sleep! While you are young, strong, wealthy, do not cease to do good! Happiness does not exist, nor should it, and if there is any meaning or purpose in life, they are not in our peddling little happiness, but in something reasonable and grand. Do good!"

Ivan Ivanich said this with a piteous supplicating smile, as though he were asking a personal favour.

Then they all three sat in different corners of the drawing-room and were silent. Ivan Ivanich's story had satisfied neither Bourkin nor Aliokhin. With the generals and ladies looking down from their gilt frames, seeming alive in the firelight, it was tedious to hear the story of a miserable official who ate gooseberries.... Somehow they had a longing to hear and to speak of charming people, and of women. And the mere fact of sitting in the drawing-room where everything—the lamp with its coloured shade, the chairs, and the carpet under their feet—told how the very people who now looked down at them from their frames once walked, and sat and had tea there, and the fact that pretty Pelagueya was near—was much better than any story.

Aliokhin wanted very much to go to bed; he had to get up for his work very early, about two in the morning, and now his eyes were closing, but he was afraid of his guests saying something interesting without his hearing it, so he would not go. He did not trouble to think whether what Ivan Ivanich had been saying was clever or right; his guests were talking of neither groats, nor hay, nor tar, but of something which had no bearing on his life, and he liked it and wanted them to go on....

"However, it's time to go to bed," said Bourkin, getting up. "I will wish you good night."

Aliokhin said good night and went down-stairs, and left his guests. Each had a large room with an old wooden bed and carved ornaments; in the corner was an ivory crucifix; and their wide, cool beds, made by pretty Pelagueya, smelled sweetly of clean linen.

Ivan Ivanich undressed in silence and lay down.

"God forgive me, a wicked sinner," he murmured, as he drew the clothes over his head.

A smell of burning tobacco came from his pipe which lay on the table, and Bourkin could not sleep for a long time and was worried because he could not make out where the unpleasant smell came from.

The rain beat against the windows all night long.

IN EXILE

OLD Simeon, whose nickname was Brains, and a young Tartar, whose name nobody knew, were sitting on the bank of the river by a wood-fire. The other three ferrymen were in the hut. Simeon who was an old man of about sixty, skinny and toothless, but broad-shouldered and healthy, was drunk. He would long ago have gone to bed, but he had a bottle in his pocket and was afraid of his comrades asking him for vodka. The Tartar was ill and miserable, and, pulling his rags about him, he went on talking about the good things in the province of Simbirsk, and what a beautiful and clever wife he had left at home. He was not more than twenty-five, and now, by the light of the wood-fire, with his pale, sorrowful, sickly face, he looked a mere boy.

"Of course, it is not a paradise here," said Brains, "you see, water, the bare bushes by the river, clay everywhere—nothing else.... It is long past Easter and there is still ice on the water and this morning there was snow...."

"Bad! Bad!" said the Tartar with a frightened look.

A few yards away flowed the dark, cold river, muttering, dashing against the holes in the clayey banks as it tore along to the distant sea. By the bank they were sitting on, loomed a great barge, which the ferrymen call a karbass. Far away and away, flashing out, flaring up, were fires crawling like snakes—last year's grass being burned. And behind the water again was darkness. Little banks of ice could be heard knocking against the barge.... It was very damp and cold....

The Tartar glanced at the sky. There were as many stars as at home, and the darkness was the same, but something was missing. At home in the Simbirsk province the stars and the sky were altogether different.

"Bad! Bad!" he repeated.

"You will get used to it," said Brains with a laugh. "You are young yet and foolish; the milk is hardly dry on your lips, and in your folly you imagine that there is no one unhappier than you, but there will come a time when you will say: God give every one such a life! Just look at me. In a week's time the floods will be gone, and we will fix the ferry here, and all of you will go away into Siberia and I shall stay here, going to and fro. I have been living thus for the last two-and-twenty years, but, thank God, I want nothing. God give everybody such a life."

The Tartar threw some branches onto the fire, crawled near to it and said:

"My father is sick. When he dies, my mother and my wife have promised to come here."

"What do you want your mother and your wife for?" asked Brains. "Just foolishness, my friend. It's the devil tempting you, plague take him. Don't listen to the Evil One. Don't give way to him. When he talks to you about women you should answer him sharply: 'I don't want them!' When he talks of freedom, you should stick to it and say: 'I don't want it. I want nothing! No father, no mother, no wife, no freedom, no home, no love! I want nothing.' Plague take 'em all."

Brains took a swig at his bottle and went on:

"My brother, I am not an ordinary peasant. I don't come from the servile masses. I am the son of a deacon, and when I was a free man at Rursk, I used to wear a frock coat, and now I have brought myself to such a point that I can sleep naked on the ground and eat grass. God give such a life to everybody. I want nothing. I am afraid of nobody and I think there is no man richer or freer than I. When they sent me here from Russia I set my teeth at once and said: 'I want nothing!' The devil whispers to me about my wife and my kindred, and about freedom and I say to him: 'I want nothing!' I stuck to it, and, you see, I live happily and have nothing to grumble at. If a man gives the devil the least opportunity and listens to him just once, then he is lost and has no hope of salvation: he will be over ears in the mire and will never get out. Not only peasants the like of you are lost, but the nobly born and the educated also. About fifteen years ago a certain nobleman was sent here from Russia. He had had some trouble with his brothers and had made a forgery in a will. People said he was a prince or a baron, but perhaps he was only a high official—who knows? Well, he came here and at once bought a house and land in Moukhzyink. 'I want to live by my own work,' said he, 'in the sweat of my brow, because I am no longer a nobleman but an exile.' 'Why,' said I. 'God help you, for that is good.' He was a young man then, ardent and eager; he used to mow and go fishing, and he would ride sixty miles on horseback. Only one thing was wrong; from the very beginning he was always driving to the post-office at Guyrin. He used to sit in my boat and sigh: 'Ah! Simeon, it is a long time since they sent me any money from home.' 'You are better without money, Vassili Sergnevich,' said I. 'What's the good of it? You just throw away the past, as though it had never happened, as though it were only a dream, and start life afresh. Don't listen to the devil,' I said, 'he won't do you any good, and he will only tighten the noose. You want money now, but in a little while you will want something else, and then more and more. If,' said I, 'you want to be happy you must want nothing. Exactly.... If,' I said, 'fate has been hard on you and me, it is no good asking her for charity and falling at her feet. We must ignore her and laugh at her.' That's what I said to him.... Two years later I ferried him over and he rubbed his hands and laughed. 'I'm going,' said he, 'to Guyrin to meet my wife. She has taken pity on me, she says, and she is coming here. She is very kind and good.' And he gave a gasp of joy. Then one day he came with his wife, a beautiful young lady with a little girl in her arms and a lot of luggage. And Vassili Andreich kept turning and looking at her and could not look at her or praise her enough. 'Yes, Simeon, my friend, even in Siberia people live.' Well, thought I, all right, you won't be content. And from that time on, mark you, he used to go to Guyrin every week to find out if money had been sent from Russia. A terrible lot of money was wasted. 'She stays here,' said he, 'for my sake, and her youth and beauty wither away here in Siberia. She shares my bitter lot with me,' said he, 'and I must give her all the pleasure I can for it....' To make his wife happier he took up with the officials and any kind of rubbish. And they couldn't have company without giving food and drink, and they must have a piano and a fluffy little dog on the sofa—bad cess to it.... Luxury, in a word, all kinds of tricks. My lady did not stay with him long. How could she? Clay, water, cold, no vegetables, no fruit; uneducated people and drunkards, with no manners, and she was a pretty pampered young lady from the metropolis.... Of course she got bored. And her husband was no longer a gentleman, but an exile—quite a different matter. Three years later, I remember, on the eve of the Assumption, I heard shouts from the other bank. I went over in the ferry and saw my lady, all wrapped up, with a young gentleman, a government official, in a troika.... I ferried them across, they got into the carriage and disappeared, and I saw no more of them. Toward the morning Vassili Andreich came racing up in a coach and pair. 'Has my wife been across, Simeon, with a gentleman in spectacles?' 'She has,' said I, 'but you might as well look for the wind in the fields.' He

40

raced after them and kept it up for five days and nights. When he came back he jumped on to the ferry and began to knock his head against the side and to cry aloud. 'You see,' said I, 'there you are.' And I laughed and reminded him: 'Even in Siberia people live.' But he went on beating his head harder than ever.... Then he got the desire for freedom. His wife had gone to Russia and he longed to go there to see her and take her away from her lover. And he began to go to the post-office every day, and then to the authorities of the town. He was always sending applications or personally handing them to the authorities, asking to have his term remitted and to be allowed to go, and he told me that he had spent over two hundred roubles on telegrams. He sold his land and mortgaged his house to the money-lenders. His hair went grey, he grew round-shouldered, and his face got yellow and consumptive-looking. He used to cough whenever he spoke and tears used to come to his eyes. He spent eight years on his applications, and at last he became happy again and lively: he had thought of a new dodge. His daughter, you see, had grown up. He doted on her and could never take his eyes off her. And, indeed, she was very pretty, dark and clever. Every Sunday he used to go to church with her at Guyrin. They would stand side by side on the ferry, and she would smile and he would devour her with his eyes. 'Yes, Simeon,' he would say. 'Even in Siberia people live. Even in Siberia there is happiness. Look what a fine daughter I have. You wouldn't find one like her in a thousand miles' journey.' 'She's a nice girl,' said I. 'Oh, yes.' ... And I thought to myself: 'You wait.... She is young. Young blood will have its way; she wants to live and what life is there here?' And she began to pine away.... Wasting, wasting away, she withered away, fell ill and had to keep to her bed.... Consumption. That's Siberian happiness, plague take it; that's Siberian life.... He rushed all over the place after the doctors and dragged them home with him. If he heard of a doctor or a quack three hundred miles off he would rush off after him. He spent a terrific amount of money on doctors and I think it would have been much better spent on drink. All the same she had to die. No help for it. Then it was all up with him. He thought of hanging himself, and of trying to escape to Russia. That would be the end of him. He would try to escape: he would be caught, tried, penal servitude, flogging."

"Good! Good!" muttered the Tartar with a shiver.

"What is good?" asked Brains.

"Wife and daughter. What does penal servitude and suffering matter? He saw his wife and his daughter. You say one should want nothing. But nothing—is evil! His wife spent three years with him. God gave him that. Nothing is evil, and three years is good. Why don't you understand that?"

Trembling and stammering as he groped for Russian words, of which he knew only a few, the Tartar began to say: "God forbid he should fall ill among strangers, and die and be buried in the cold sodden earth, and then, if his wife could come to him if only for one day or even for one hour, he would gladly endure any torture for such happiness, and would even thank God. Better one day of happiness than nothing."

Then once more he said what a beautiful clever wife he had left at home, and with his head in his hands he began to cry and assured Simeon that he was innocent, and had been falsely accused. His two brothers and his uncle had stolen some horses from a peasant and beat the old man nearly to death, and the community never looked into the matter at all, and judgment was passed by which all three brothers were exiled to Siberia, while his uncle, a rich man, remained at home.

"You will get used to it," said Simeon.

The Tartar relapsed into silence and stared into the fire with his eyes red from weeping; he looked perplexed and frightened, as if he could not understand why he was in the cold and the darkness, among strangers, and not in the province of Simbirsk. Brains lay down near the fire, smiled at something, and began to say in an undertone:

"But what a joy she must be to your father," he muttered after a pause. "He loves her and she is a comfort to him, eh? But, my man, don't tell me. He is a strict, harsh old man. And girls don't want strictness; they want kisses and laughter, scents and pomade. Yes.... Ah! What a life!" Simeon swore heavily. "No more vodka! That means bedtime. What? I'm going, my man."

Left alone, the Tartar threw more branches on the fire, lay down, and, looking into the blaze, began to think of his native village and of his wife; if she could come if only for a month, or even a day, and then, if she liked, go back again! Better a month or even a day, than nothing. But even if his wife kept her promise and came, how could he provide for her? Where was she to live?

"If there is nothing to eat; how are we to live?" asked the Tartar aloud.

For working at the oars day and night he was paid two copecks a day; the passengers gave tips, but the ferrymen shared them out and gave nothing to the Tartar, and only laughed at him. And he was poor, cold, hungry, and fearful.... With his whole body aching and shivering he thought it would be good to go into the hut and sleep; but there was nothing to cover himself with, and it was colder there than on the bank. He had nothing to cover himself with there, but he could make up a fire....

In a week's time, when the floods had subsided and the ferry would be fixed up, all the ferrymen except Simeon would not be wanted any longer and the Tartar would have to go from village to village, begging and looking for work. His wife was only seventeen; beautiful, soft, and shy.... Could she go unveiled begging through the villages? No. The idea of it was horrible.

It was already dawn. The barges, the bushy willows above the water, the swirling flood began to take shape, and up above in a clayey cliff a hut thatched with straw, and above that the straggling houses of the village, where the cocks had begun to crow.

The ginger-coloured clay cliff, the barge, the river, the strange wild people, hunger, cold, illness—perhaps all these things did not really exist. Perhaps, thought the Tartar, it was only a dream. He felt that he must be asleep, and he heard his own snoring.... Certainly he was at home in the Simbirsk province; he had but to call his wife and she would answer; and his mother was in the next room.... But what awful dreams there are! Why? The Tartar smiled and opened his eyes. What river was that? The Volga?

It was snowing.

"Hi! Ferry!" some one shouted on the other bank. "Karba-a-ass!"

The Tartar awoke and went to fetch his mates to row over to the other side. Hurrying into their sheepskins, swearing sleepily in hoarse voices, and shivering from the cold, the four men appeared on the bank. After their sleep, the river from which there came a piercing blast, seemed to them horrible and disgusting. They stepped slowly into the barge.... The Tartar and the three ferrymen took the long, broad-bladed oars, which in the dim light looked like a crab's claw, and Simeon flung himself with his belly against the tiller. And on the other side the voice kept on shouting, and a revolver was fired twice, for the man probably thought the ferrymen were asleep or gone to the village inn.

"All right. Plenty of time!" said Brains in the tone of one who was convinced that there is no need for hurry in this world—and indeed there is no reason for it.

The heavy, clumsy barge left the bank and heaved through the willows, and by the willows slowly receding it was possible to tell that the barge was moving. The ferrymen plied the oars with a slow measured stroke; Brains hung over the tiller with his stomach pressed against it and swung from side to side. In the dim light they looked like men sitting on some antediluvian animal with long limbs, swimming out to a cold dismal nightmare country.

They got clear of the willows and swung out into mid-stream. The thud of the oars and the splash could be heard on the other bank and shouts came: "Quicker! Quicker!" After another ten minutes the barge bumped heavily against the landing-stage.

"And it is still snowing, snowing all the time," Simeon murmured, wiping the snow off his face. "God knows where it comes from!"

On the other side a tall, lean old man was waiting in a short fox-fur coat and a white astrachan hat. He was standing some distance from his horses and did not move; he had a stern concentrated expression as if he were trying to remember something and were furious with his recalcitrant memory. When Simeon went up to him and took off his hat with a smile he said:

"I'm in a hurry to get to Anastasievka. My daughter is worse again and they tell me there's a new doctor at Anastasievka."

The coach was clamped onto the barge and they rowed back. All the while as they rowed the man, whom Simeon called Vassili Andreich, stood motionless, pressing his thick lips tight and staring in front of him. When the driver craved leave to smoke in his presence, he answered nothing, as if he did not hear. And Simeon hung over the rudder and looked at him mockingly and said:

"Even in Siberia people live. L-i-v-e!"

On Brains's face was a triumphant expression as if he were proving something, as if pleased that things had happened just as he thought they would. The unhappy, helpless look of the man in the fox-fur coat seemed to give him great pleasure.

"The roads are now muddy, Vassili Andreich," he said, when the horses had been harnessed on the bank. "You'd better wait a couple of weeks, until it gets dryer.... If there were any point in going—but you know yourself that people are always on the move day and night and there's no point in it. Sure!"

Vassili Andreich said nothing, gave him a tip, took his seat in the coach and drove away.

"Look! He's gone galloping after the doctor!" said Simeon, shivering in the cold. "Yes. To look for a real doctor, trying to overtake the wind in the fields, and catch the devil by the tail, plague take him! What queer fish there are! God forgive me, a miserable sinner."

The Tartar went up to Brains, and, looking at him with mingled hatred and disgust, trembling, and mixing Tartar words up with his broken Russian, said:

"He good ... good. And you ... bad! You are bad! The gentleman is a good soul, very good, and you are a beast, you are bad! The gentleman is alive and you are dead.... God made man that he should be alive, that he should have happiness, sorrow, grief, and you want nothing, so you are not alive, but a stone! A stone wants nothing and so do you.... You are a stone—and God does not love you and the gentleman he does."

They all began to laugh: the Tartar furiously knit his brows, waved his hand, drew his rags round him and went to the fire. The ferrymen and Simeon went slowly to the hut.

"It's cold," said one of the ferrymen hoarsely, as he stretched himself on the straw with which the damp, clay floor was covered.

"Yes. It's not warm," another agreed.... "It's a hard life."

All of them lay down. The wind blew the door open. The snow drifted into the hut. Nobody could bring himself to get up and shut the door; it was cold, but they put up with it.

"And I am happy," muttered Simeon as he fell asleep. "God give such a life to everybody."

"You certainly are the devil's own. Even the devil don't need to take you."

Sounds like the barking of a dog came from outside.

"Who is that? Who is there?"

"It's the Tartar crying."

"Oh! he's a queer fish."

"He'll get used to it!" said Simeon, and at once he fell asleep. Soon the others slept too and the door was left open.

THE LADY WITH THE TOY DOG

I

*J*T was reported that a new face had been seen on the quay; a lady with a little dog. Dimitri Dimitrich Gomov, who had been a fortnight at Talta and had got used to it, had begun to show an interest in new faces. As he sat in the pavilion at Verné's he saw a young lady, blond and fairly tall, and wearing a broad-brimmed hat, pass along the quay. After her ran a white Pomeranian.

Later he saw her in the park and in the square several times a day. She walked by herself, always in the same broad-brimmed hat, and with this white dog. Nobody knew who she was, and she was spoken of as the lady with the toy dog.

"If," thought Gomov, "if she is here without a husband or a friend, it would be as well to make her acquaintance."

He was not yet forty, but he had a daughter of twelve and two boys at school. He had married young, in his second year at the University, and now his wife seemed half as old again as himself. She was a tall woman, with dark eyebrows, erect, grave, stolid, and she thought herself an intellectual woman. She read a great deal, called her husband not Dimitri, but Demitri, and in his private mind he thought her short-witted, narrow-minded, and ungracious. He was afraid of her and disliked being at home. He had begun to betray her with other women long ago, betrayed her frequently, and, probably for that reason nearly always spoke ill of women, and when they were discussed in his presence he would maintain that they were an inferior race.

It seemed to him that his experience was bitter enough to give him the right to call them any name he liked, but he could not live a couple of days without the "inferior race." With men he was bored and ill at ease, cold and unable to talk, but when he was with women, he felt easy and knew what to talk about, and how to behave, and even when he was silent with them he felt quite comfortable. In his appearance as in his character, indeed in his whole nature, there was something attractive, indefinable, which drew women to him and charmed them; he knew it, and he, too, was drawn by some mysterious power to them.

His frequent, and, indeed, bitter experiences had taught him long ago that every affair of that kind, at first a divine diversion, a delicious smooth adventure, is in the end a source of worry for a decent man, especially for men like those at Moscow who are slow to move, irresolute, domesticated, for it becomes at last an acute and extraordinary complicated problem and a nuisance. But whenever he met and was interested in a new woman, then his experience would slip away from his memory, and he would long to live, and everything would seem so simple and amusing.

And it so happened that one evening he dined in the gardens, and the lady in the broad-brimmed hat came up at a leisurely pace and sat at the next table. Her expression, her gait, her dress, her coiffure told him that she belonged to society, that she was married, that she was paying her first visit to Talta, that she was alone, and that she was bored.... There is a great deal of untruth in the gossip about the immorality of the place. He scorned such tales, knowing that they were for the most part concocted by people who would be only too ready to sin if they had the chance, but when the lady sat down at the next table, only a yard or two away from him, his thoughts were filled with tales of easy conquests, of trips to the mountains; and he was suddenly possessed by the alluring idea of a quick transitory liaison, a moment's affair with an unknown woman whom he knew not even by name.

He beckoned to the little dog, and when it came up to him, wagged his finger at it. The dog began to growl. Gomov again wagged his finger.

The lady glanced at him and at once cast her eyes down.

"He won't bite," she said and blushed.

"May I give him a bone?"—and when she nodded emphatically, he asked affably: "Have you been in Talta long?"

"About five days."

"And I am just dragging through my second week."

They were silent for a while.

"Time goes quickly," she said, "and it is amazingly boring here."

"It is the usual thing to say that it is boring here. People live quite happily in dull holes like Bieliev or Zhidra, but as soon as they come here they say: 'How boring it is! The very dregs of dullness!' One would think they came from Spain."

She smiled. Then both went on eating in silence as though they did not know each other; but after dinner they went off together—and then began an easy, playful conversation as though they were perfectly happy, and it was all one to them where they went or what they talked of. They walked and talked of how the sea was strangely luminous; the water lilac, so soft and warm, and athwart it the moon cast a golden streak. They said how stifling it was after the hot day. Gomov told her how he came from Moscow and was a philologist by education, but in a bank by profession; and how he had once wanted to sing in opera, but gave it up; and how he had two houses in Moscow.... And from her he learned that she came from Petersburg, was born there, but married at S. where she had been living for the last two years; that she would stay another month at Talta, and perhaps her husband would come for her, because he too, needed a rest. She could not tell him what her husband was—Provincial Administration or Zemstvo Council—and she seemed to think it funny. And Gomov found out that her name was Anna Sergueyevna.

In his room at night, he thought of her and how they would meet next day. They must do so. As he was going to sleep, it struck him that she could only lately have left school, and had been at her lessons even as his daughter was then; he remembered how bashful and gauche she was when she laughed and talked with a stranger—it must be, he thought, the first time she had been alone, and in such a place with men walking after her and looking at her and talking to her, all with the same secret purpose which she could not but guess. He thought of her slender white neck and her pretty, grey eyes.

"There is something touching about her," he thought as he began to fall asleep.

II

A week passed. It was a blazing day. Indoors it was stifling, and in the streets the dust whirled along. All day long he was plagued with thirst and he came into the pavilion every few minutes and offered Anna Sergueyevna an iced drink or an ice. It was impossibly hot.

In the evening, when the air was fresher, they walked to the jetty to see the steamer come in. There was quite a crowd all gathered to meet somebody, for they carried bouquets. And among them were clearly marked the peculiarities of Talta: the elderly ladies were youngly dressed and there were many generals.

The sea was rough and the steamer was late, and before it turned into the jetty it had to do a great deal of manœuvring. Anna Sergueyevna looked through her lorgnette at the steamer and the passengers as though she were looking for friends, and when she turned to Gomov, her eyes shone. She talked much and her questions were abrupt, and she forgot what she had said; and then she lost her lorgnette in the crowd.

The well-dressed people went away, the wind dropped, and Gomov and Anna Sergueyevna stood as though they were waiting for somebody to come from the steamer. Anna Sergueyevna was silent. She smelled her flowers and did not look at Gomov.

"The weather has got pleasanter toward evening," he said. "Where shall we go now? Shall we take a carriage?"

She did not answer.

He fixed his eyes on her and suddenly embraced her and kissed her lips, and he was kindled with the perfume and the moisture of the flowers; at once he started and looked round; had not some one seen?

"Let us go to your—" he murmured.

And they walked quickly away.

Her room was stifling, and smelled of scents which she had bought at the Japanese shop. Gomov looked at her and thought: "What strange chances there are in life!" From the past there came the memory of earlier good-natured women, gay in their love, grateful to him for their happiness, short though it might be; and of others—like his wife—who loved without sincerity, and talked overmuch and affectedly, hysterically, as though they were protesting that it was not love, nor passion, but something more important; and of the few beautiful cold women, into whose eyes there would flash suddenly a fierce expression, a stubborn desire to take, to snatch from life more than it can give; they were no longer in their first youth, they were capricious, unstable, domineering, imprudent, and when Gomov became cold toward them then their beauty roused him to hatred, and the lace on their lingerie reminded him of the scales of fish.

But here there was the shyness and awkwardness of inexperienced youth, a feeling of constraint; an impression of perplexity and wonder, as though some one had suddenly knocked at the door. Anna Sergueyevna, "the lady with the toy dog" took what had happened somehow seriously, with a particular gravity, as though thinking that this was her downfall and very strange and improper. Her features seemed to sink and wither, and on either side of her face her long hair hung mournfully down; she sat crestfallen and musing, exactly like a woman taken in sin in some old picture.

"It is not right," she said. "You are the first to lose respect for me."

There was a melon on the table. Gomov cut a slice and began to eat it slowly. At least half an hour passed in silence.

Anna Sergueyevna was very touching; she irradiated the purity of a simple, devout, inexperienced woman; the solitary candle on the table hardly lighted her face, but it showed her very wretched.

"Why should I cease to respect you?" asked Gomov. "You don't know what you are saying."

"God forgive me!" she said, and her eyes filled with tears. "It is horrible."

"You seem to want to justify yourself."

"How can I justify myself? I am a wicked, low woman and I despise myself. I have no thought of justifying myself. It is not my husband that I have deceived, but myself. And not only now but for a long time past. My husband may be a good honest man, but he is a lackey. I do not know what work he does, but I do know that he is a lackey in his soul. I was twenty when I married him. I was overcome by curiosity. I longed for something. 'Surely,' I said to myself, 'there is another kind of life.' I longed to live! To live, and to live.... Curiosity burned me up.... You do not understand it, but I swear by God, I could no longer control myself. Something strange was going on in me. I could not hold myself in. I told my husband that I was ill and came here.... And here I have been walking about dizzily, like a lunatic.... And now I have become a low, filthy woman whom everybody may despise."

Gomov was already bored; her simple words irritated him with their unexpected and inappropriate repentance; but for the tears in her eyes he might have thought her to be joking or playing a part.

"I do not understand," he said quietly. "What do you want?"

She hid her face in his bosom and pressed close to him.

"Believe, believe me, I implore you," she said. "I love a pure, honest life, and sin is revolting to me. I don't know myself what I am doing. Simple people say: 'The devil entrapped me,' and I can say of myself: 'The Evil One tempted me.'"

"Don't, don't," he murmured.

He looked into her staring, frightened eyes, kissed her, spoke quietly and tenderly, and gradually quieted her and she was happy again, and they both began to laugh.

Later, when they went out, there was not a soul on the quay; the town with its cypresses looked like a city of the dead, but the sea still roared and broke against the shore; a boat swung on the waves; and in it sleepily twinkled the light of a lantern.

They found a cab and drove out to the Oreanda.

"Just now in the hall," said Gomov, "I discovered your name

written on the board—von Didenitz. Is your husband a German?"

"No. His grandfather, I believe, was a German, but he himself is an Orthodox Russian."

At Oreanda they sat on a bench, not far from the church, looked down at the sea and were silent. Talta was hardly visible through the morning mist. The tops of the hills were shrouded in motionless white clouds. The leaves of the trees never stirred, the cicadas trilled, and the monotonous dull sound of the sea, coming up from below, spoke of the rest, the eternal sleep awaiting us. So the sea roared when there was neither Talta nor Oreanda, and so it roars and will roar, dully, indifferently when we shall be no more. And in this continual indifference to the life and death of each of us, lives pent up, the pledge of our eternal salvation, of the uninterrupted movement of life on earth and its unceasing perfection. Sitting side by side with a young woman, who in the dawn seemed so beautiful, Gomov, appeased and enchanted by the sight of the fairy scene, the sea, the mountains, the clouds, the wide sky, thought how at bottom, if it were thoroughly explored, everything on earth was beautiful, everything, except what we ourselves think and do when we forget the higher purposes of life and our own human dignity.

A man came up—a coast-guard—gave a look at them, then went away. He, too, seemed mysterious and enchanted. A steamer came over from Feodossia, by the light of the morning star, its own lights already put out.

"There is dew on the grass," said Anna Sergueyevna after a silence.

"Yes. It is time to go home."

They returned to the town.

Then every afternoon they met on the quay, and lunched together, dined, walked, enjoyed the sea. She complained that she slept badly, that her heart beat alarmingly. She would ask the same question over and over again, and was troubled now by jealousy, now by fear that he did not sufficiently respect her. And often in the square or the gardens, when there was no one near, he would draw her close and kiss her passionately. Their complete idleness, these kisses in the full daylight, given timidly and fearfully lest any one should see, the heat, the smell of the sea and the continual brilliant parade of leisured, well-dressed, well-fed people almost regenerated him. He would tell Anna Sergueyevna how delightful she was, how tempting. He was impatiently passionate, never left her side, and she would often brood, and even asked him to confess that he did not respect her, did not love her at all, and only saw in her a loose woman. Almost every evening, rather late, they would drive out of the town, to Oreanda, or to the waterfall; and these drives were always delightful, and the impressions won during them were always beautiful and sublime.

They expected her husband to come. But he sent a letter in which he said that his eyes were bad and implored his wife to come home. Anna Sergueyevna began to worry.

"It is a good thing I am going away," she would say to Gomov. "It is fate."

She went in a carriage and he accompanied her. They drove for a whole day. When she took her seat in the car of an express-train and when the second bell sounded, she said:

"Let me have another look at you.... Just one more look. Just as you are."

She did not cry, but was sad and low-spirited, and her lips trembled.

"I will think of you—often," she said. "Good-bye. Good-bye. Don't think ill of me. We part for ever. We must, because we ought not to have met at all. Now, good-bye."

The train moved off rapidly. Its lights disappeared, and in a minute or two the sound of it was lost, as though everything were agreed to put an end to this sweet, oblivious madness. Left alone on the platform, looking into the darkness, Gomov heard the trilling of the grasshoppers and the humming of the telegraph-wires, and felt as though he had just woke up. And he thought that it had been one more adventure, one more affair, and it also was finished and had left only a memory. He was moved, sad, and filled with a faint remorse; surely the young woman, whom he would never see again, had not been happy with him; he had been kind to her, friendly, and sincere, but still in his attitude toward her, in his tone and caresses, there had always been a thin shadow of raillery, the rather rough arrogance of the successful male aggravated by the fact that he was twice as old as she. And all the time she had called him kind, remarkable, noble, so that he was never really himself to her, and had involuntarily deceived her....

Here at the station, the smell of autumn was in the air, and the evening was cool.

"It is time for me to go North," thought Gomov, as he left the platform. "It is time."

III

At home in Moscow, it was already like winter; the stoves were heated, and in the mornings, when the children were getting ready to go to school, and had their tea, it was dark and their nurse lighted the lamp for a short while. The frost had already begun. When the first snow falls, the first day of driving in sledges, it is good to see the white earth, the white roofs; one breathes easily, eagerly, and then one remembers the days of youth. The old lime-trees and birches, white with hoarfrost, have a kindly expression; they are nearer to the heart than cypresses and palm-trees, and with the dear familiar trees there is no need to think of mountains and the sea.

Gomov was a native of Moscow. He returned to Moscow on a fine frosty day, and when he donned his fur coat and warm gloves, and took a stroll through Petrovka, and when on Saturday evening he heard the church-bells ringing, then his recent travels and the places he had visited lost all their charm. Little by little he sank back into Moscow life, read eagerly three newspapers a day, and said that he did not read Moscow papers as a matter of principle. He was drawn into a round of restaurants, clubs, dinner-parties, parties, and he was flattered to have his house frequented by famous lawyers and actors, and to play cards with a professor at the University club. He could eat a whole plateful of hot sielianka.

So a month would pass, and Anna Sergueyevna, he thought, would be lost in the mists of memory and only rarely would she visit his dreams with her touching smile, just as other women had done. But more than a month passed, full winter came, and in his memory everything was clear, as though he had parted from Anna Sergueyevna only yesterday. And his memory was lit by a light that grew ever stronger. No matter how, through the voices of his children saying their lessons, penetrating to the evening stillness of his study, through hearing a song, or the music in a restaurant, or the snow-storm howling in the chimney, suddenly the whole thing would come to life again in his memory: the meeting on the jetty, the early morning with the mists on the mountains, the steamer from Feodossia and their kisses. He would pace up and down his room and remember it all and smile, and then his memories would drift into dreams, and the past was confused in his imagination with the future. He did not dream at night of Anna Sergueyevna, but she followed him everywhere, like a shadow, watching him. As he shut his eyes, he could see her, vividly, and she seemed handsomer, tenderer, younger than in reality; and he seemed to himself better than he had been at Talta. In the evenings she would look at him from the bookcase, from the fireplace, from the corner; he could hear her breathing and the soft rustle of her dress. In the street he would gaze at women's faces to see if there were not one like her....

He was filled with a great longing to share his memories with some one. But at home it was impossible to speak of his love, and away from home—there was no one. Impossible to talk of her to the other people in the house and the men at the bank. And talk of what? Had he loved then? Was there anything fine, romantic, or elevating or even interesting in his relations with Anna Sergueyevna? And he would speak vaguely of love, of women, and nobody guessed what was the matter, and only his wife would raise her dark eyebrows and say:

"Demitri, the rôle of coxcomb does not suit you at all."

One night, as he was coming out of the club with his partner, an official, he could not help saying:

"If only I could tell what a fascinating woman I met at Talta."

The official seated himself in his sledge and drove off, but suddenly called:

"Dimitri Dimitrich!"

"Yes."

"You were right. The sturgeon was tainted."

These banal words suddenly roused Gomov's indignation. They seemed to him degrading and impure. What barbarous customs and people!

What preposterous nights, what dull, empty days! Furious card-playing, gourmandising, drinking, endless conversations about the same things, futile activities and conversations taking up the best part of the day and all the best of a man's forces, leaving only a stunted, wingless life, just rubbish; and to go away and escape was impossible—one might as well be in a lunatic asylum or in prison with hard labour.

Gomov did not sleep that night, but lay burning with indignation, and then all next day he had a headache. And the following night he slept badly, sitting up in bed and thinking, or pacing from corner to corner of his room. His children bored him, the bank bored him, and he had no desire to go out or to speak to any one.

In December when the holidays came he prepared to go on a journey and told his wife he was going to Petersburg to present a petition for a young friend of his—and went to S. Why? He did not know. He wanted to see Anna Sergueyevna, to talk to her, and if possible to arrange an assignation.

He arrived at S. in the morning and occupied the best room in the hotel, where the whole floor was covered with a grey canvas, and on the table there stood an inkstand grey with dust, adorned with a horseman on a headless horse holding a net in his raised hand. The porter gave him the necessary information: von Dide-nitz; Old Goucharno Street, his own house—not far from the ho-tel; lives well, has his own horses, every one knows him.

Gomov walked slowly to Old Goucharno Street and found the house. In front of it was a long, grey fence spiked with nails.

"No getting over a fence like that," thought Gomov, glancing from the windows to the fence.

He thought: "To-day is a holiday and her husband is probably at home. Besides it would be tactless to call and upset her. If he sent a note then it might fall into her husband's hands and spoil everything. It would be better to wait for an opportunity." And he kept on walking up and down the street, and round the fence, waiting for his opportunity. He saw a beggar go in at the gate and the dogs attack him. He heard a piano and the sounds came faint-ly to his ears. It must be Anna Sergueyevna playing. The door suddenly opened and out of it came an old woman, and after her ran the familiar white Pomeranian. Gomov wanted to call the dog, but his heart suddenly began to thump and in his agitation he could not remember the dog's name.

He walked on, and more and more he hated the grey fence and thought with a gust of irritation that Anna Sergueyevna had al-ready forgotten him, and was perhaps already amusing herself with some one else, as would be only natural in a young wom-an forced from morning to night to behold the accursed fence. He returned to his room and sat for a long time on the sofa, not knowing what to do. Then he dined and afterward slept for a long while.

"How idiotic and tiresome it all is," he thought as he awoke and saw the dark windows; for it was evening. "I've had sleep enough, and what shall I do to-night?"

He sat on his bed which was covered with a cheap, grey blanket, exactly like those used in a hospital, and tormented himself.

"So much for the lady with the toy dog.... So much for the great adventure.... Here you sit."

However, in the morning, at the station, his eye had been caught by a poster with large letters: "First Performance of 'The Geisha.'" He remembered that and went to the theatre.

"It is quite possible she will go to the first performance," he thought.

The theatre was full and, as usual in all provincial theatres, there was a thick mist above the lights, the gallery was noisily restless; in the first row before the opening of the performance stood the local dandies with their hands behind their backs, and there in the governor's box, in front, sat the governor's daughter, and the governor himself sat modestly behind the curtain and only his hands were visible. The curtain quivered; the orchestra tuned up for a long time, and while the audience were coming in and taking their seats, Gomov gazed eagerly round.

At last Anna Sergueyevna came in. She took her seat in the third row, and when Gomov glanced at her his heart ached and he knew that for him there was no one in the whole world nearer, dearer, and more important than she; she was lost in this provincial rabble, the little undistinguished woman, with a common lorgnette in her hands, yet she filled his whole life; she was his grief, his joy, his only happiness, and he longed for her; and through the noise of the bad orchestra with its tenth-rate fiddles, he thought how dear she was to him. He thought and dreamed.

With Anna Sergueyevna there came in a young man with short side-whiskers, very tall, stooping; with every movement he shook and bowed continually. Probably he was the husband whom in a bitter mood at Talta she had called a lackey. And, indeed, in his long figure, his side-whiskers, the little bald patch on the top of his head, there was something of the lackey; he had a modest sugary smile and in his buttonhole he wore a University badge exactly like a lackey's number.

In the first entr'acte the husband went out to smoke, and she was left alone. Gomov, who was also in the pit, came up to her and said in a trembling voice with a forced smile:

"How do you do?"

She looked up at him and went pale. Then she glanced at him again in terror, not believing her eyes, clasped her fan and lorgnette tightly together, apparently struggling to keep herself from fainting. Both were silent. She sat, he stood; frightened by her emotion, not daring to sit down beside her. The fiddles and flutes began to play and suddenly it seemed to them as though all the people in the boxes were looking at them. She got up and walked quickly to the exit; he followed, and both walked absently along the corridors, down the stairs, up the stairs, with the crowd shifting and shimmering before their eyes; all kinds of uniforms, judges, teachers, crown-estates, and all with badges; ladies shone and shimmered before them, like fur coats on moving rows of clothes-pegs, and there was a draught howling through the place laden with the smell of tobacco and cigar-ends. And Gomov, whose heart was thudding wildly, thought:

"Oh, Lord! Why all these men and that beastly orchestra?"

At that very moment he remembered how when he had seen Anna Sergueyevna off that evening at the station he had said to himself that everything was over between them, and they would never meet again. And now how far off they were from the end!

On a narrow, dark staircase over which was written: "This Way to the Amphitheatre," she stopped:

"How you frightened me!" she said, breathing heavily, still pale and apparently stupefied. "Oh! how you frightened me! I am nearly dead. Why did you come? Why?"

"Understand me, Anna," he whispered quickly. "I implore you to understand...."

She looked at him fearfully, in entreaty, with love in her eyes, gazing fixedly to gather up in her memory every one of his features.

"I suffer so!" she went on, not listening to him. "All the time, I thought only of you. I lived with thoughts of you.... And I wanted to forget, to forget, but why, why did you come?"

A little above them, on the landing, two schoolboys stood and smoked and looked down at them, but Gomov did not care. He drew her to him and began to kiss her cheeks, her hands.

"What are you doing? What are you doing?" she said in terror, thrusting him away.... "We were both mad. Go away to-night. You must go away at once.... I implore you, by everything you hold sacred, I implore you.... The people are coming——"

Some one passed them on the stairs.

"You must go away," Anna Sergueyevna went on in a whisper. "Do you hear, Dimitri Dimitrich? I'll come to you in Moscow. I never was happy. Now I am unhappy and I shall never, never be happy, never! Don't make me suffer even more! I swear, I'll come to Moscow. And now let us part. My dear, dearest darling, let us part!"

She pressed his hand and began to go quickly down-stairs, all the while looking back at him, and in her eyes plainly showed that she was most unhappy. Gomov stood for a while, listened, then, when all was quiet he found his coat and left the theatre.

IV

And Anna Sergueyevna began to come to him in Moscow. Once every two or three months she would leave S., telling her husband that she was going to consult a specialist in women's diseases. Her husband half believed and half disbelieved her. At Moscow she would stay at the "Slaviansky Bazaar" and send a message at once to Gomov. He would come to her, and nobody in Moscow knew.

Once as he was going to her as usual one winter morning—he had not received her message the night before—he had his daughter with him, for he was taking her to school which was on the way. Great wet flakes of snow were falling.

"Three degrees above freezing," he said, "and still the snow is falling. But the warmth is only on the surface of the earth. In the upper strata of the atmosphere there is quite a different temperature."

"Yes, papa. Why is there no thunder in winter?"

He explained this too, and as he spoke he thought of his assignation, and that not a living soul knew of it, or ever would know. He had two lives; one obvious, which every one could see and know, if they were sufficiently interested, a life full of conventional truth and conventional fraud, exactly like the lives of his friends and acquaintances; and another, which moved underground. And by a strange conspiracy of circumstances, everything that was to him important, interesting, vital, everything that enabled him to be sincere and denied self-deception and was the very core of his being, must dwell hidden away from others, and everything that made him false, a mere shape in which he hid himself in order to conceal the truth, as for instance his work in the bank, arguments at the club, his favourite gibe about women, going to parties with his wife—all this was open. And, judging others by himself, he did not believe the things he saw, and assumed that everybody else also had his real vital life passing under a veil of mystery as under the cover of the night. Every man's intimate existence is kept mysterious, and perhaps, in part, because of that civilised people are so nervously anxious that a personal secret should be respected.

When he had left his daughter at school, Gomov went to the "Slaviansky Bazaar." He took off his fur coat down-stairs, went up and knocked quietly at the door. Anna Sergueyevna, wearing his favourite grey dress, tired by the journey, had been expecting him to come all night. She was pale, and looked at him without a smile, and flung herself on his breast as soon as he entered. Their kiss was long and lingering as though they had not seen each other for a couple of years.

"Well, how are you getting on down there?" he asked. "What is your news?"

"Wait. I'll tell you presently.... I cannot."

She could not speak, for she was weeping. She turned her face from him and dried her eyes.

"Well, let her cry a bit.... I'll wait," he thought, and sat down.

Then he rang and ordered tea, and then, as he drank it, she stood and gazed out of the window.... She was weeping in distress, in the bitter knowledge that their life had fallen out so sadly; only seeing each other in secret, hiding themselves away like thieves! Was not their life crushed?

"Don't cry.... Don't cry," he said.

It was clear to him that their love was yet far from its end, which there was no seeing. Anna Sergueyevna was more and more passionately attached to him; she adored him and it was inconceivable that he should tell her that their love must some day end; she would not believe it.

He came up to her and patted her shoulder fondly and at that moment he saw himself in the mirror.

His hair was already going grey. And it seemed strange to him that in the last few years he should have got so old and ugly. Her shoulders were warm and trembled to his touch. He was suddenly filled with pity for her life, still so warm and beautiful, but probably beginning to fade and wither, like his own. Why should she love him so much? He always seemed to women not what he really was, and they loved in him, not himself, but the creature of their imagination, the thing they hankered for in life, and when they had discovered their mistake, still they loved him. And not one of them was happy with him. Time passed; he met women and was friends with them, went further and parted, but never once did he love; there was everything but love.

And now at last when his hair was grey he had fallen in love, real love—for the first time in his life.

Anna Sergueyevna and he loved one another, like dear kindred, like husband and wife, like devoted friends; it seemed to them that Fate had destined them for one another, and it was inconceivable that he should have a wife, she a husband; they were like two birds of passage, a male and a female, which had been caught and forced to live in separate cages. They had forgiven each other all the past of which they were ashamed; they forgave everything in the present, and they felt that their love had changed both of them.

Formerly, when he felt a melancholy compunction, he used to comfort himself with all kinds of arguments, just as they happened to cross his mind, but now he was far removed from any such ideas; he was filled with a profound pity, and he desired to be tender and sincere....

"Don't cry, my darling," he said. "You have cried enough.... Now let us talk and see if we can't find some way out."

Then they talked it all over, and tried to discover some means of avoiding the necessity for concealment and deception, and the torment of living in different towns, and of not seeing each other for a long time. How could they shake off these intolerable fetters?

"How? How?" he asked, holding his head in his hands. "How?"

And it seemed that but a little while and the solution would be found and there would begin a lovely new life; and to both of them it was clear that the end was still very far off, and that their hardest and most difficult period was only just beginning.

GOUSSIEV

I

*J*T was already dark and would soon be night.

Goussiev, a private on long leave, raised himself a little in his hammock and said in a whisper:

"Can you hear me, Pavel Ivanich? A soldier at Souchan told me that their boat ran into an enormous fish and knocked a hole in her bottom."

The man of condition unknown whom he addressed, and whom everybody in the hospital-ship called Pavel Ivanich, was silent, as if he had not heard.

And once more there was silence.... The wind whistled through the rigging, the screw buzzed, the waves came washing, the hammocks squeaked, but to all these sounds their ears were long since accustomed and it seemed as though everything were wrapped in sleep and silence. It was very oppressive. The three patients—two soldiers and a sailor—who had played cards all day were now asleep and tossing to and fro.

The vessel began to shake. The hammock under Goussiev slowly heaved up and down, as though it were breathing—one, two, three.... Something crashed on the floor and began to tinkle: the jug must have fallen down.

"The wind has broken loose...." said Goussiev, listening attentively.

This time Pavel Ivanich coughed and answered irritably:

"You spoke just now of a ship colliding with a large fish, and now you talk of the wind breaking loose.... Is the wind a dog to break loose?"

"That's what people say."

"Then people are as ignorant as you.... But what do they not say? You should keep a head on your shoulders and think. Silly idiot!"

Pavel Ivanich was subject to seasickness. When the ship rolled he would get very cross, and the least trifle would upset him, though Goussiev could never see anything to be cross about. What was there unusual in his story about the fish or in his saying that the wind had broken loose? Suppose the fish were as big as a mountain and its back were as hard as a sturgeon's, and suppose that at the end of the wood there were huge stone walls with the snarling winds chained up to them.... If they do not break loose, why then do they rage over the sea as though they were possessed, and rush about like dogs? If they are not chained, what happens to them when it is calm?

Goussiev thought for a long time of a fish as big as a mountain, and of thick rusty chains; then he got tired of that and began to think of his native place whither he was returning after five years' service in the Far East. He saw with his mind's eye the great pond covered with snow.... On one side of the pond was a brick-built pottery, with a tall chimney belching clouds of black smoke, and on the other side was the village.... From the yard of the fifth house from the corner came his brother Alency in a sledge; behind him sat his little son Vanka in large felt boots, and his daughter Akulka, also in felt boots. Alency is tipsy, Vanka laughs, and Akulka's face is hidden—she is well wrapped up.

"The children will catch cold ..." thought Goussiev. "God grant them," he whispered, "a pure right mind that they may honour their parents and be better than their father and mother...."

"The boots want soling," cried the sick sailor in a deep voice. "Aye, aye."

The thread of Goussiev's thoughts was broken, and instead of the pond, suddenly—without rhyme or reason—he saw a large bull's head without eyes, and the horse and sledge did not move on, but went round and round in a black mist. But still he was glad he had seen his dear ones. He gasped for joy, and his limbs tingled and his fingers throbbed.

"God suffered me to see them!" he muttered, and opened his eyes and looked round in the darkness for water.

He drank, then lay down again, and once more the sledge skimmed along, and he saw the bull's head without eyes, black smoke, clouds of it. And so on till dawn.

II

At first through the darkness there appeared only a blue circle, the port-hole, then Goussiev began slowly to distinguish the man in the next hammock, Pavel Ivanich. He was sleeping in a sitting position, for if he lay down he could not breathe. His face was grey; his nose long and sharp, and his eyes were huge, because he was so thin; his temples were sunk, his beard scanty, the hair on his head long.... By his face it was impossible to tell his class:

gentleman, merchant, or peasant; judging by his appearance and long hair he looked almost like a recluse, a lay-brother, but when he spoke—he was not at all like a monk. He was losing strength through his cough and his illness and the suffocating heat, and he breathed heavily and was always moving his dry lips. Noticing that Goussiev was looking at him, he turned toward him and said:

"I'm beginning to understand.... Yes.... Now I understand."

"What do you understand, Pavel Ivanich?"

"Yes.... It was strange to me at first, why you sick men, instead of being kept quiet, should be on this steamer, where the heat is stifling, and stinking, and pitching and tossing, and must be fatal to you; but now it is all clear to me.... Yes. The doctors sent you to the steamer to get rid of you. They got tired of all the trouble you gave them, brutes like you.

...You don't pay them; you only give a lot of trouble, and if you die you spoil their reports. Therefore you are just cattle, and there is no difficulty in getting rid of you.... They only need to lack conscience and humanity, and to deceive the owners of the steamer. We needn't worry about the first, they are experts by nature; but the second needs a certain amount of practice. In a crowd of four hundred healthy soldiers and sailors—five sick men are never noticed; so you were carried up to the steamer, mixed with a healthy lot who were counted in such a hurry that nothing wrong was noticed, and when the steamer got away they saw fever-stricken and consumptive men lying helpless on the deck...."

Goussiev could not make out what Pavel Ivanich was talking about; thinking he was being taken to task, he said by way of excusing himself:

"I lay on the deck because when we were taken off the barge I caught a chill."

"Shocking!" said Pavel Ivanich. "They know quite well that you can't last out the voyage, and yet they send you here! You may get as far as the Indian Ocean, but what then? It is awful to think of.... And that's all the return you get for faithful unblemished service!"

Pavel Ivanich looked very angry, and smote his forehead and gasped:

"They ought to be shown up in the papers. There would be an awful row."

The two sick soldiers and the sailor were already up and had begun to play cards, the sailor propped up in his hammock, and the soldiers squatting uncomfortably on the floor. One soldier had his right arm in a sling and his wrist was tightly bandaged so that he had to hold the cards in his left hand or in the crook of his elbow. The boat was rolling violently so that it was impossible to get up or to drink tea or to take medicine.

"You were an orderly?" Pavel Ivanich asked Goussiev.

"That's it. An orderly."

"My God, my God!" said Pavel Ivanich sorrowfully. "To take a man from his native place, drag him fifteen thousand miles, drive him into consumption ... and what for? I ask you. To make him an orderly to some Captain Farthing or Midshipman Hole! Where's the sense of it?"

"It's not a bad job, Pavel Ivanich. You get up in the morning, clean the boots, boil the samovar, tidy up the room, and then there is nothing to do. The lieutenant draws plans all day long, and you can pray to God if you like—or read books—or go out into the streets. It's a good enough life."

"Yes. Very good! The lieutenant draws plans, and you stay in the kitchen all day long and suffer from homesickness.... Plans.... Plans don't matter. It's human life that matters! Life doesn't come again. One should be sparing of it."

"Certainly Pavel Ivanich. A bad man meets no quarter, either at home, or in the army, but if you live straight, and do as you are told, then no one will harm you. They are educated and they understand.... For five years now I've never been in the cells and I've only been thrashed once—touch wood!"

"What was that for?"

"Fighting. I have a heavy fist, Pavel Ivanich. Four Chinamen came into our yard: they were carrying wood, I think, but I don't remember. Well, I was bored. I went for them and one of them got a bloody nose. The lieutenant saw it through the window and gave me a thick ear."

"You poor fool," muttered Pavel Ivanich. "You don't understand anything."

He was completely exhausted with the tossing of the boat and shut his eyes; his head fell back and then flopped forward onto his chest. He tried several times to lie down, but in vain, for he could not breathe.

"And why did you go for the four Chinamen?" he asked after a while.

"For no reason. They came into the yard and I went for them."

Silence fell.... The gamblers played for a couple of hours, absorbed and cursing, but the tossing of the ship tired even them; they threw the cards away and laid down. Once more Goussiev

64

thought of the big pond, the pottery, the village. Once more the sledges skimmed along, once more Vanka laughed, and that fool of an Akulka opened her fur coat, and stretched out her feet; look, she seemed to say, look, poor people, my felt boots are new and not like Vanka's.

"She's getting on for six and still she has no sense!" said Goussiev. "Instead of showing your boots off, why don't you bring some water to your soldier-uncle? I'll give you a present."

Then came Andrea, with his firelock on his shoulder, carrying a hare he had shot, and he was followed by Tsaichik the cripple, who offered him a piece of soap for the hare; and there was the black heifer in the yard, and Domna sewing a shirt and crying over something, and there was the eyeless bull's head and the black smoke....

Overhead there was shouting, sailors running; the sound of something heavy being dragged along the deck, or something had broken.... More running. Something wrong? Goussiev raised his head, listened and saw the two soldiers and the sailor playing cards again; Pavel Ivanich sitting up and moving his lips. It was very close, he could hardly breathe, he wanted a drink, but the water was warm and disgusting.... The pitching of the boat was now better.

Suddenly something queer happened to one of the soldiers.... He called ace of diamonds, lost his reckoning and dropped his cards. He started and laughed stupidly and looked round.

"In a moment, you fellows," he said and lay down on the floor.

All were at a loss. They shouted at him but he made no reply.

"Stiepan, are you ill?" asked the other soldier with the bandaged hand. "Perhaps we'd better call the priest, eh?"

"Stiepan, drink some water," said the sailor. "Here, mate, have a drink."

"What's the good of breaking his teeth with the jug," shouted Goussiev angrily. "Don't you see, you fatheads?"

"What."

"What!" cried Goussiev. "He's snuffed it, dead. That's what! Good God, what fools!..."

III

The rolling stopped and Pavel Ivanich cheered up. He was no longer peevish. His face had an arrogant, impetuous, and mocking expression. He looked as if he were on the point of saying: "I'll tell you a story that will make you die of laughter." Their porthole was open and a soft wind blew in on Pavel Ivanich. Voices could be heard and the splash of oars in the water.... Beneath the window some one was howling in a thin, horrible voice; probably a Chinaman singing.

"Yes. We are in harbour," said Pavel Ivanich, smiling mockingly. "Another month and we shall be in Russia. It's true; my gallant warriors, I shall get to Odessa and thence I shall go straight to Kharkhov. At Kharkhov I have a friend, a literary man. I shall go to him and I shall say, 'now, my friend, give up your rotten little love-stories and descriptions of nature, and expose the vileness of the human biped.... There's a subject for you.'"

He thought for a moment and then he said:

"Goussiev, do you know how I swindled them?"

"Who, Pavel Ivanich?"

"The lot out there.... You see there's only first and third class on the steamer, and only peasants are allowed to go third. If you have a decent suit, and look like a nobleman or a bourgeois, at a distance, then you must go first. It may break you, but you have to lay down your five hundred roubles. 'What's the point of such an arrangement?' I asked. 'Is it meant to raise the prestige of Russian intellectuals?' 'Not a bit,' said they. 'We don't let you go, simply because it is impossible for a decent man to go third. It is so vile and disgusting.' 'Yes,' said I. 'Thanks for taking so much trouble about decent people. Anyhow, bad or no, I haven't got five hundred roubles as I have neither robbed the treasury nor exploited foreigners, nor dealt in contraband, nor flogged any one to death, and, therefore, I think I have a right to go first-class and to take rank with the intelligentsia of Russia.' But there's no convincing them by logic.... I had to try fraud. I put on a peasant's coat and long boots, and a drunken, stupid expression and went to the agent and said: 'Give me a ticket, your Honour.'

"'What's your position?' says the agent.

"'Clerical,' said I. 'My father was an honest priest. He always told the truth to the great ones of the earth, and so he suffered much.'"

Pavel Ivanich got tired with talking, and his breath failed him, but he went on:

"Yes. I always tell the truth straight out.... I am afraid of nobody and nothing. There's a great difference between myself and you in that respect. You are dull, blind, stupid, you see nothing, and you don't understand what you do see. You are told that the wind breaks its chain, that you are brutes and worse, and you believe; you are thrashed and you kiss the hand that thrashes you; a swine in a raccoon pelisse robs you, and throws you sixpence for tea, and you say: 'Please, your Honour, let me kiss your hand.' You are pariahs, skunks.... I am different. I live consciously. I see everything, as an eagle or a hawk sees when it hovers over the earth, and I understand everything. I am a living protest. I see injustice—I protest; I see bigotry and hypocrisy—I protest; I see swine triumphant—I protest, and I am unconquerable. No Spanish inquisition can make me hold my tongue. Aye.... Cut my tongue out. I'll protest by gesture.... Shut me up in a dungeon—I'll shout so loud that I shall be heard for a mile round, or I'll starve myself, so that there shall be a still heavier weight on their black consciences. Kill me—and my ghost will return. All my acquaintances tell me: 'You are a most insufferable man, Pavel Ivanich!' I am proud of such a reputation. I served three years in the Far East, and have got bitter memories enough for a hundred years. I inveighed against it all. My friends write from Russia: 'Do not come.' But I'm going, to spite them.... Yes.... That is life. I understand. You can call that life."

Goussiev was not listening, but lay looking out of the port-hole; on the transparent lovely turquoise water swung a boat all shining in the shimmering light; a fat Chinaman was sitting in it eating rice with chop-sticks. The water murmured softly, and over it lazily soared white sea-gulls.

"It would be fun to give that fat fellow one on the back of his neck...." thought Goussiev, watching the fat Chinaman and yawning.

He dozed, and it seemed to him that all the world was slumbering. Time slipped swiftly away. The day passed imperceptibly; imperceptibly the twilight fell.... The steamer was still no longer but was moving on.

IV

Two days passed. Pavel Ivanich no longer sat up, but lay full length; his eyes were closed and his nose seemed to be sharper than ever.

"Pavel Ivanich!" called Goussiev, "Pavel Ivanich."

Pavel Ivanich opened his eyes and moved his lips.

"Aren't you well?"

"It's nothing," answered Pavel Ivanich, breathing heavily. "It's nothing. No. I'm much better. You see I can lie down now. I'm much better."

"Thank God for it, Pavel Ivanich."

"When I compare myself with you, I am sorry for you ... poor devils. My lungs are all right; my cough comes from indigestion

... I can endure this hell, not to mention the Red Sea! Besides, I have a critical attitude toward my illness, as well as to my medicine. But you ... you are ignorant.... It's hard lines on you, very hard."

The ship was running smoothly; it was calm but still stifling and hot as a Turkish bath; it was hard not only to speak but even to listen without an effort. Goussiev clasped his knees, leaned his head on them and thought of his native place. My God, in such heat it was a pleasure to think of snow and cold! He saw himself driving on a sledge, and suddenly the horses were frightened and bolted.... Heedless of roads, dikes, ditches they rushed like mad through the village, across the pond, past the works, through the fields.... "Hold them in!" cried the women and the passers-by. "Hold them in!" But why hold them in? Let the cold wind slap your face and cut your hands; let the lumps of snow thrown up by the horses' hoofs fall on your hat, down your neck and chest; let the runners of the sledge be buckled, and the traces and harness be torn and be damned to it! What fun when the sledge topples over and you are flung hard into a snow-drift; with your face slap into the snow, and you get up all white with your moustaches covered with icicles, hatless, gloveless, with your belt undone.... People laugh and dogs bark....

Pavel Ivanich, with one eye half open looked at Goussiev and asked quietly:

"Goussiev, did your commander steal?"

"How do I know, Pavel Ivanich? The likes of us don't hear of it."

A long time passed in silence. Goussiev thought, dreamed, drank water; it was difficult to speak, difficult to hear, and he was afraid of being spoken to. One hour passed, a second, a third; evening came, then night; but he noticed nothing as he sat dreaming of the snow.

He could hear some one coming into the ward; voices, but five minutes passed and all was still.

"God rest his soul!" said the soldier with the bandaged hand. "He was a restless man."

"What?" asked Goussiev. "Who?"

"He's dead. He has just been taken up-stairs."

"Oh, well," muttered Goussiev with a yawn. "God rest his soul."

"What do you think, Goussiev?" asked the bandaged soldier after some time. "Will he go to heaven?"

"Who?"

"Pavel Ivanich."

"He will. He suffered much. Besides, he was a priest's son, and priests have many relations. They will pray for his soul."

The bandaged soldier sat down on Goussiev's hammock and said in an undertone:

"You won't live much longer, Goussiev. You'll never see Russia."

"Did the doctor or the nurse tell you that?" asked Goussiev.

"No one told me, but I can see it. You can always tell when a man is going to die soon. You neither eat nor drink, and you have gone very thin and awful to look at. Consumption. That's what it is. I'm not saying this to make you uneasy, but because I thought you might like to have the last sacrament. And if you have any money, you had better give it to the senior officer."

"I have not written home," said Goussiev. "I shall die and they will never know."

"They will know," said the sailor in his deep voice. "When you die they will put you down in the log, and at Odessa they will give a note to the military governor, and he will send it to your parish or wherever it is...."

This conversation made Goussiev begin to feel unhappy and a vague desire began to take possession of him. He drank water—it was not that; he stretched out to the port-hole and breathed the hot, moist air—it was not that; he tried to think of his native place and the snow—it was not that.... At last he felt that he would choke if he stayed a moment longer in the hospital.

"I feel poorly, mates," he said. "I want to go on deck. For Christ's sake take me on deck."

Goussiev flung his arms round the soldier's neck and the soldier held him with his free arm and supported him up the gangway. On deck there were rows and rows of sleeping soldiers and sailors; so many of them that it was difficult to pick a way through them.

"Stand up," said the bandaged soldier gently. "Walk after me slowly and hold on to my shirt...."

It was dark. There was no light on deck or on the masts or over the sea. In the bows a sentry stood motionless as a statue, but he looked as if he were asleep. It was as though the steamer had been left to its own sweet will, to go where it liked.

"They are going to throw Pavel Ivanich into the sea," said the bandaged soldier. "They will put him in a sack and throw him overboard."

"Yes. That's the way they do."

"But it's better to lie at home in the earth. Then the mother can go to the grave and weep over it."

"Surely."

There was a smell of dung and hay. With heads hanging there were oxen standing by the bulwark—one, two, three ... eight beasts. And there was a little horse. Goussiev put out his hand to pat it, but it shook its head, showed its teeth and tried to bite his sleeve.

"Damn you," said Goussiev angrily.

He and the soldier slowly made their way to the bows and stood against the bulwark and looked silently up and down. Above them was the wide sky, bright with stars, peace and tranquillity—exactly as it was at home in his village; but below—darkness and turbulence. Mysterious towering waves. Each wave seemed to strive to rise higher than the rest; and they pressed and jostled each other and yet others came, fierce and ugly, and hurled themselves into the fray.

There is neither sense nor pity in the sea. Had the steamer been smaller, and not made of tough iron, the waves would have crushed it remorselessly and all the men in it, without distinction of good and bad. The steamer too seemed cruel and senseless. The large-nosed monster pressed forward and cut its way through millions of waves; it was afraid neither of darkness, nor of the wind, nor of space, nor of loneliness; it cared for nothing, and if the ocean had its people, the monster would crush them without distinction of good and bad.

"Where are we now?" asked Goussiev.

"I don't know. Must be the ocean."

"There's no land in sight."

"Why, they say we shan't see land for another seven days."

The two soldiers looked at the white foam gleaming with phosphorescence. Goussiev was the first to break the silence.

"Nothing is really horrible," he said. "You feel uneasy, as if you were in a dark forest. Suppose a boat were lowered and I was ordered to go a hundred miles out to sea to fish—I would go. Or suppose I saw a soul fall into the water—I would go in after him. I wouldn't go in for a German or a Chinaman, but I'd try to save a Russian."

"Aren't you afraid to die?"

"Yes. I'm afraid. I'm sorry for the people at home. I have a brother at home, you know, and he is not steady; he drinks, beats his wife for nothing at all, and my old father and mother may be brought to ruin. But my legs are giving way, mate, and it is hot here.... Let me go to bed."

V

Goussiev went back to the ward and lay down in his hammock. As before, a vague desire tormented him and he could not make out what it was. There was a congestion in his chest; a noise in his head, and his mouth was so dry that he could hardly move his tongue. He dozed and dreamed, and, exhausted by the heat, his cough and the nightmares that haunted him, toward morning he fell into a deep sleep. He dreamed he was in barracks, and the bread had just been taken out of the oven, and he crawled into the oven and lathered himself with a birch broom. He slept for two days and on the third day in the afternoon two sailors came down and carried him out of the ward.

He was sewn up in sail-cloth, and to make him heavier two iron bars were sewn up with him. In the sail-cloth he looked like a carrot or a radish, broad at the top, narrow at the bottom.... Just before sunset he was taken on deck and laid on a board one end of which lay on the bulwark, the other on a box, raised up by a stool. Round him stood the invalided soldiers.

"Blessed is our God," began the priest; "always, now and for ever and ever."

"Amen!" said three sailors.

The soldiers and the crew crossed themselves and looked askance at the waves. It was strange that a man should be sewn up in sail-cloth and dropped into the sea. Could it happen to any one?

The priest sprinkled Goussiev with earth and bowed. A hymn was sung.

The guard lifted up the end of the board, Goussiev slipped down it; shot headlong, turned over in the air, then plop! The foam covered him, for a moment it looked as though he was swathed in lace, but the moment passed—and he disappeared beneath the waves.

He dropped down to the bottom. Would he reach it? The bottom is miles down, they say. He dropped down almost sixty or seventy feet, then began to go slower and slower, swung to and fro as though he were thinking; then, borne along by the current; he moved more sideways than downward.

But soon he met a shoal of pilot-fish. Seeing a dark body, the fish stopped dead and sudden, all together, turned and went back. Less than a minute later, like arrows they darted at Goussiev, zig-zagging through the water around him....

Later came another dark body, a shark. Gravely and leisurely, as though it had not noticed Goussiev, it swam up under him, and he rolled over on its back; it turned its belly up, taking its ease in the warm, translucent water, and slowly opened its mouth with its two rows of teeth. The pilot-fish were wildly excited; they stopped to see what was going to happen. The shark played with the body, then slowly opened its mouth under it, touched it with its teeth, and the sail-cloth was ripped open from head to foot; one of the bars fell out, frightening the pilot-fish and striking the shark on its side, and sank to the bottom.

And above the surface, the clouds were huddling up about the setting sun; one cloud was like a triumphal arch, another like a lion, another like a pair of scissors.... From behind the clouds came a broad green ray reaching up to the very middle of the sky; a little later a violet ray was flung alongside this, and then others gold and pink.... The sky was soft and lilac, pale and tender. At first beneath the lovely, glorious sky the ocean frowned, but soon the ocean also took on colour—sweet, joyful, passionate colours, almost impossible to name in human language.

MY LIFE

I

THE STORY OF A PROVINCIAL

THE director said to me: "I only keep you out of respect for your worthy father, or you would have gone long since." I replied: "You flatter me, your Excellency, but I suppose I am in a position to go." And then I heard him saying: "Take the fellow away, he is getting on my nerves."

Two days later I was dismissed. Ever since I had been grown up, to the great sorrow of my father, the municipal architect, I had changed my position nine times, going from one department to another, but all the departments were as like each other as drops of water; I had to sit and write, listen to inane and rude remarks, and just wait until I was dismissed.

When I told my father, he was sitting back in his chair with his eyes shut. His thin, dry face, with a dove-coloured tinge where he shaved (his face was like that of an old Catholic organist), wore an expression of meek submission. Without answering my greeting or opening his eyes, he said:

"If my dear wife, your mother, were alive, your life would be a constant grief to her. I can see the hand of Providence in her untimely death. Tell me, you unhappy boy," he went on, opening his eyes, "what am I to do with you?"

When I was younger my relations and friends knew what to do with me; some advised me to go into the army as a volunteer, others were for pharmacy, others for the telegraph service; but now that I was twenty-four and was going grey at the temples and had already tried the army and pharmacy and the telegraph service, and every possibility seemed to be exhausted, they gave me no more advice, but only sighed and shook their heads.

"What do you think of yourself?" my father went on. "At your age other young men have a good social position, and just look at yourself: a lazy lout, a beggar, living on your father!"

And, as usual, he went on to say that young men were going to the dogs through want of faith, materialism, and conceit, and that amateur theatricals should be prohibited because they seduce young people from religion and their duty.

"To-morrow we will go together, and you shall apologise to the director and promise to do your work conscientiously," he concluded. "You must not be without a position in society for a single day."

"Please listen to me," said I firmly, though I did not anticipate gaining anything by speaking. "What you call a position in society is the privilege of capital and education. But people who are poor and uneducated have to earn their living by hard physical labour, and I see no reason why I should be an exception."

"It is foolish and trivial of you to talk of physical labour," said my father with some irritation. "Do try to understand, you idiot, and get it into your brainless head, that in addition to physical strength you have a divine spirit; a sacred fire, by which you are distinguished from an ass or a reptile and bringing you nigh to God. This sacred fire has been kept alight for thousands of years by the best of mankind. Your great-grandfather, General Pologniev, fought at Borodino; your grandfather was a poet, an orator, and a marshal of the nobility; your uncle was an educationalist; and I, your father, am an architect! Have all the Polognievs kept the sacred fire alight for you to put it out?"

"There must be justice," said I. "Millions of people have to do manual labour."

"Let them. They can do nothing else! Even a fool or a criminal can do manual labour. It is the mark of a slave and a barbarian, whereas the sacred fire is given only to a few!"

It was useless to go on with the conversation. My father worshipped himself and would not be convinced by anything unless he said it himself. Besides, I knew quite well that the annoyance with which he spoke of unskilled labour came not so much from any regard for the sacred fire, as from a secret fear that I should become a working man and the talk of the town. But the chief thing was that all my schoolfellows had long ago gone through the University and were making careers for themselves, and the son of the director of the State Bank was already a collegiate assessor, while I, an only son, was nothing! It was useless and unpleasant to go on with the conversation, but I still sat there and raised objections in the hope of making myself understood. The problem was simple and clear: how was I to earn my living? But he could not see its simplicity and kept on talking with sugary rounded phrases about Borodino and the sacred fire, and my uncle, and the forgotten poet who wrote bad, insincere verses, and he called me a brainless fool. But how I longed to be understood! In spite of everything, I loved my father and my sister, and from boyhood I have had a habit of considering them, so strongly rooted that I shall probably never get rid of it; whether I am right or wrong I am always afraid of hurting them, and go in terror lest my father's thin neck should go red with anger and he should have an apoplectic fit.

"It is shameful and degrading for a man of my age to sit in a stuffy room and compete with a typewriting-machine," I said. "What has that to do with the sacred fire?"

"Still, it is intellectual work," said my father. "But that's enough. Let us drop the conversation and I warn you that if you refuse to return to your office and indulge your contemptible inclinations, then you will lose my love and your sister's. I shall cut you out of my will—that I swear, by God!"

With perfect sincerity, in order to show the purity of my motives, by which I hope to be guided all through my life, I said:

"The matter of inheritance does not strike me as important. I renounce any rights I may have."

For some unexpected reason these words greatly offended my father. He went purple in the face.

"How dare you talk to me like that, you fool!" he cried to me in a thin, shrill voice. "You scoundrel!" And he struck me quickly and dexterously with a familiar movement; once—twice. "You forget yourself!"

When I was a boy and my father struck me, I used to stand bolt upright like a soldier and look him straight in the face; and, exactly as if I were still a boy, I stood erect, and tried to look into his eyes. My father was old and very thin, but his spare muscles must have been as strong as whip-cord, for he hit very hard.

I returned to the hall, but there he seized his umbrella and struck me several times over the head and shoulders; at that moment my sister opened the drawing-room door to see what the noise was, but immediately drew back with an expression of pity and horror, and said not one word in my defence.

My intention not to return to the office, but to start a new working life, was unshakable. It only remained to choose the kind of work—and there seemed to be no great difficulty about that, because I was strong, patient, and willing. I was prepared to face a monotonous, laborious life, of semi-starvation, filth, and rough surroundings, always overshadowed with the thought of finding a job and a living. And—who knows—returning from work in the Great Gentry Street, I might often envy Dolyhikov, the engineer, who lives by intellectual work, but I was happy in thinking of my coming troubles. I used to dream of intellectual activity, and to imagine myself a teacher, a doctor, a writer, but my dreams remained only dreams. A liking for intellectual pleasures—like the theatre and reading—grew into a passion with me, but I did not know whether I had any capacity for intellectual work. At school I had an unconquerable aversion for the Greek language, so that I had to leave when I was in the fourth class. Teachers were got to coach me up for the fifth class, and then I went into various departments, spending most of my time in perfect idleness, and this, I was told, was intellectual work.

My activity in the education department or in the municipal office required neither mental effort, nor talent, nor personal ability, nor creative spiritual impulse; it was purely mechanical, and such intellectual work seemed to me lower than manual labour. I despise it and I do not think that it for a moment justifies an idle, careless life, because it is nothing but a swindle, and only a kind of idleness. In all probability I have never known real intellectual work.

It was evening. We lived in Great Gentry Street—the chief street in the town—and our rank and fashion walked up and down it in the evenings, as there were no public gardens. The street was very charming, and was almost as good as a garden, for it had two rows of poplar-trees, which smelt very sweet, especially after rain, and acacias, and tall trees, and apple-trees hung over the fences and hedges. May evenings, the scent of the lilac, the hum of the cockchafers, the warm, still air—how new and extraordinary it all is, though spring comes every year! I stood by the gate and looked at the passers-by. With most of them I had grown up and had played with them, but now my presence might upset them, because I was poorly dressed, in unfashionable clothes, and people made fun of my very narrow trousers and large, clumsy boots, and called them macaroni-on-steamboats. And I had a bad reputation in the town because I had no position and went to play billiards in low cafés, and had once been taken up, for no particular offence, by the political police.

In a large house opposite, Dolyhikov's, the engineer's, some one was playing the piano. It was beginning to get dark and the stars were beginning to shine. And slowly, answering people's salutes, my father passed with my sister on his arm. He was wearing an old top hat with a broad curly brim.

"Look!" he said to my sister, pointing to the sky with the very umbrella with which he had just struck me. "Look at the sky!

Even the smallest stars are worlds! How insignificant man is in comparison with the universe."

And he said this in a tone that seemed to convey that he found it extremely flattering and pleasant to be so insignificant. What an untalented man he was! Unfortunately, he was the only architect in the town, and during the last fifteen or twenty years I could not remember one decent house being built. When he had to design a house, as a rule he would draw first the hall and the drawing-room; as in olden days schoolgirls could only begin to dance by the fireplace, so his artistic ideas could only evolve from the hall and drawing-room. To them he would add the dining-room, nursery, study, connecting them with doors, so that in the end they were just so many passages, and each room had two or three doors too many. His houses were obscure, extremely confused, and limited. Every time, as though he felt something was missing, he had recourse to various additions, plastering them one on top of the other, and there would be various lobbies, and passages, and crooked staircases leading to the entresol, where it was only possible to stand in a stooping position, and where instead of a floor there would be a thin flight of stairs like a Russian bath, and the kitchen would always be under the house with a vaulted ceiling and a brick floor. The front of his houses always had a hard, stubborn expression, with stiff, French lines, low, squat roofs, and fat, pudding-like chimneys surmounted with black cowls and squeaking weathercocks. And somehow all the houses built by my father were like each other, and vaguely reminded me of a top hat, and the stiff, obstinate back of his head. In the course of time the people of the town grew used to my father's lack of talent, which took root and became our style.

My father introduced the style into my sister's life. To begin with, he gave her the name of Cleopatra (and he called me Misail). When she was a little girl he used to frighten her by telling her about the stars and our ancestors; and explained the nature of life and duty to her at great length; and now when she was twenty-six he went on in the same way, allowing her to take no one's arm but his own, and somehow imagining that sooner or later an ardent young man would turn up and wish to enter into marriage with her out of admiration for his qualities. And she adored my father, was afraid of him, and believed in his extraordinary intellectual powers.

It got quite dark and the street grew gradually empty. In the house opposite the music stopped. The gate was wide open and out into the street, careering with all its bells jingling, came a troika. It was the engineer and his daughter going for a drive. Time to go to bed!

I had a room in the house, but I lived in the courtyard in a hut, under the same roof as the coach-house, which had been built probably as a harness-room—for there were big nails in the walls—but now it was not used, and my father for thirty years had kept his newspapers there, which for some reason he had bound half-yearly and then allowed no one to touch. Living there I was less in touch with my father and his guests, and I used to think that if I did not live in a proper room and did not go to the house every day for meals, my father's reproach that I was living on him lost some of its sting.

My sister was waiting for me. She had brought me supper unknown to my father; a small piece of cold veal and a slice of bread. In the family there were sayings: "Money loves an account," or "A copeck saves a rouble," and so on, and my sister, impressed by such wisdom, did her best to cut down expenses and made us feed rather meagrely. She put the plate on the table, sat on my bed, and began to cry.

"Misail," she said, "what are you doing to us?"

She did not cover her face, her tears ran down her cheeks and hands, and her expression was sorrowful. She fell on the pillow, gave way to her tears, trembling all over and sobbing.

"You have left your work again!" she said. "How awful!"

"Do try to understand, sister!" I said, and because she cried I was filled with despair.

As though it were deliberately arranged, the paraffin in my little lamp ran out, and the lamp smoked and guttered, and the old hooks in the wall looked terrible and their shadows flickered.

"Spare us!" said my sister, rising up. "Father is in an awful state, and I am ill. I shall go mad. What will become of you?" she asked, sobbing and holding out her hands to me. "I ask you, I implore you, in the name of our dear mother, to go back to your work."

"I cannot, Cleopatra," I said, feeling that only a little more would make me give in. "I cannot."

"Why?" insisted my sister, "why? If you have not made it up with your chief, look for another place. For instance, why shouldn't you work on the railway? I have just spoken to Aniuta Blagovo, and she assures me you would be taken on, and she even promised to do what she could for you. For goodness sake, Misail, think! Think it over, I implore you!"

We talked a little longer and I gave in. I said that the thought of working on the railway had never come into my head, and that I was ready to try.

She smiled happily through her tears and clasped my hand, and still she cried, because she could not stop, and I went into the kitchen for paraffin.

II

Among the supporters of amateur theatricals, charity concerts, and tableaux vivants the leaders were the Azhoguins, who lived in their own house in Great Gentry house the Street. They used to lend their house and assume the necessary trouble and expense. They were a rich landowning family, and had about three thousand urskins, with a magnificent farm in the neighbourhood, but they did not care for village life and lived in the town summer and winter. The family consisted of a mother, a tall, spare, delicate lady, who had short hair, wore a blouse and a plain skirt à l'Anglais, and three daughters, who were spoken of, not by their names, but as the eldest, the middle, and the youngest; they all had ugly, sharp chins, and they were short-sighted, high-shouldered, dressed in the same style as their mother, had an unpleasant lisp, and yet they always took part in every play and were always doing something for charity—acting, reciting, singing. They were very serious and never smiled, and even in burlesque operettas they acted without gaiety and with a businesslike air, as though they were engaged in bookkeeping.

I loved our plays, especially the rehearsals, which were frequent, rather absurd, and noisy, and we were always given supper after them. I had no part in the selection of the pieces and the casting of the characters. I had to look after the stage. I used to design the scenery and copy out the parts, and prompt and make up. And I also had to look after the various effects such as thunder, the singing of a nightingale, and so on. Having no social position, I had no decent clothes, and during rehearsals had to hold aloof from the others in the darkened wings and shyly say nothing.

I used to paint the scenery in the Azhoguins' coach-house or yard. I was assisted by a house-painter, or, as he called himself, a decorating contractor, named Andrey Ivanov, a man of about fifty, tall and very thin and pale, with a narrow chest, hollow temples, and dark rings under his eyes, he was rather awful to look at. He had some kind of wasting disease, and every spring and autumn he was said to be on the point of death, but he would go to bed for a while and then get up and say with surprise: "I'm not dead this time!"

In the town he was called Radish, and people said it was his real name. He loved the theatre as much as I, and no sooner did he hear that a play was in hand than he gave up all his work and went to the Azhoguins' to paint scenery.

The day after my conversation with my sister I worked from morning till night at the Azhoguins'. The rehearsal was fixed for seven o'clock, and an hour before it began all the players were assembled, and the eldest, the middle, and the youngest Miss Azhoguin were reading their parts on the stage. Radish, in a long, brown overcoat with a scarf wound round his neck, was standing, leaning with his head against the wall, looking at the stage with a rapt expression. Mrs. Azhoguin went from guest to guest saying something pleasant to every one. She had a way of gazing into one's face and speaking in a hushed voice as though she were telling a secret.

"It must be difficult to paint scenery," she said softly, coming up to me. "I was just talking to Mrs. Mufke about prejudice when I saw you come in. Mon Dieu! All my life I have struggled against prejudice. To convince the servants that all their superstitions are nonsense I always light three candles, and I begin all my important business on the thirteenth."

The daughter of Dolyhikov, the engineer, was there, a handsome, plump, fair girl, dressed, as people said in our town, in Parisian style. She did not act, but at rehearsals a chair was put for her on the stage, and the plays did not begin until she appeared in the front row, to astonish everybody with the brilliance of her clothes. As coming from the metropolis, she was allowed to make remarks during rehearsals, and she did so with an affable, condescending smile, and it was clear that she regarded our plays as a childish amusement. It was said that she had studied singing at the Petersburg conservatoire and had sung for a winter season in opera. I liked her very much, and during rehearsals or the performance, I never took my eyes off her.

I had taken the book and began to prompt when suddenly my sister appeared. Without taking off her coat and hat she came up to me and said:

"Please come!"

I went. Behind the stage in the doorway stood Aniuta Blagovo, also wearing a hat with a dark veil. She was the daughter of the vice-president of the Court, who had been appointed to our town years ago, almost as soon as the High Court was established. She was tall and had a good figure, and was considered indispensable for the tableaux vivants, and when she represented a fairy or a muse, her face would burn with shame; but she took no part in the plays, and would only look in at rehearsals, on some business, and never enter the hall. And it was evident now that she had only looked in for a moment.

"My father has mentioned you," she said drily, not looking at me and blushing.... "Dolyhikov has promised to find you something to do on the railway. If you go to his house to-morrow, he will see you."

I bowed and thanked her for her kindness.

"And you must leave this," she said, pointing to my book.

She and my sister went up to Mrs. Azhoguin and began to whisper, looking at me.

"Indeed," said Mrs. Azhoguin, coming up to me, and gazing into my face. "Indeed, if it takes you from your more serious business"—she took the book out of my hands—"then you must hand it over to some one else. Don't worry, my friend. It will be all right."

I said good-bye and left in some confusion. As I went downstairs I saw my sister and Aniuta Blagovo going away; they were talking animatedly, I suppose about my going on the railway, and they hurried away. My sister had never been to a rehearsal before, and she was probably tortured by her conscience and by her fear of my father finding out that she had been to the Azhoguins' without permission.

The next day I went to see Dolyhikov at one o'clock. The man servant showed me into a charming room, which was the engineer's drawing-room and study. Everything in it was charming and tasteful, and to a man like myself, unused to such things, very strange. Costly carpets, huge chairs, bronzes, pictures in gold and velvet frames; photographs on the walls of beautiful women, clever, handsome faces, and striking attitudes; from the drawing-room a door led straight into the garden, by a veranda, and I saw lilac and a table laid for breakfast, rolls, and a bunch of roses; and there was a smell of spring, and good cigars, and happiness—and everything seemed to say, here lives a man who has worked and won the highest happiness here on earth. At the table the engineer's daughter was sitting reading a newspaper.

"Do you want my father?" she asked. "He is having a shower-bath. He will be down presently. Please take a chair."

I sat down.

"I believe you live opposite?" she asked after a short silence.

"Yes."

"When I have nothing to do I look out of the window. You must excuse me," she added, turning to her newspaper, "and I often see you and your sister. She has such a kind, wistful expression."

Dolyhikov came in. He was wiping his neck with a towel.

"Papa, this is Mr. Pologniev," said his daughter.

"Yes, yes. Blagovo spoke to me." He turned quickly to me, but did not hold out his hand. "But what do you think I can give you? I'm not bursting with situations. You are queer people!" he went on in a loud voice and as though he were scolding me. "I get about twenty people every day, as though I were a Department of State. I run a railway, sir. I employ hard labour; I need mechanics, navvies, joiners, well-sinkers, and you can only sit and write. That's all! You are all clerks!"

And he exhaled the same air of happiness as his carpets and chairs. He was stout, healthy, with red cheeks and a broad chest; he looked clean in his pink shirt and wide trousers, just like a china figure of a post-boy. He had a round, bristling beard—and not a single grey hair—and a nose with a slight bridge, and bright, innocent, dark eyes.

"What can you do?" he went on. "Nothing! I am an engineer and well-to-do, but before I was given this railway I worked very hard for a long time. I was an engine-driver for two years, I worked in Belgium as an ordinary lubricator. Now, my dear man, just think—what work can I offer you?"

"I quite agree," said I, utterly abashed, not daring to meet his bright, innocent eyes.

"Are you any good with the telegraph?" he asked after some thought.

"Yes. I have been in the telegraph service."

"Hm.... Well, we'll see. Go to Dubechnia. There's a fellow there already. But he is a scamp."

"And what will my duties be?" I asked.

"We'll see to that later. Go there now. I'll give orders. But please don't drivel and don't bother me with petitions or I'll kick you out."

He turned away from me without even a nod. I bowed to him and his daughter, who was reading the newspaper, and went out. I felt so miserable that when my sister asked how the engineer had received me, I could not utter a single word.

To go to Dubechnia I got up early in the morning at sunrise. There was not a soul in the street, the whole town was asleep, and my footsteps rang out with a hollow sound. The dewy poplars filled the air with a soft scent. I was sad and had no desire to leave the town. It seemed so nice and warm! I loved the green trees, the quiet sunny mornings, the ringing of the bells, but the people in the town were alien to me, tiresome and sometimes even loath-some. I neither liked nor understood them.

I did not understand why or for what purpose those thirty-five thousand people lived. I knew that Kimry made a living by man-ufacturing boots, that Tula made samovars and guns, that Odessa was a port; but I did not know what our town was or what it did. The people in Great Gentry Street and two other clean streets had independent means and salaries paid by the Treasury, but how the people lived in the other eight streets which stretched parallel to each other for three miles and then were lost behind the hill—that was always an insoluble problem to me. And I am ashamed to think of the way they lived. They had neither public gardens, nor a theatre, nor a decent orchestra; the town and club libraries are used only by young Jews, so that books and maga-zines would lie for months uncut. The rich and the intelligentsia slept in close, stuffy bedrooms, with wooden beds infested with bugs; the children were kept in filthy, dirty rooms called nurs-eries, and the servants, even when they were old and respecta-ble, slept on the kitchen floor and covered themselves with rags. Except in Lent all the houses smelt of bortsch, and during Lent of sturgeon fried in sunflower oil. The food was unsavoury, the water unwholesome. On the town council, at the governor's, at the archbishop's, everywhere there had been talk for years about there being no good, cheap water-supply and of borrowing two hundred thousand roubles from the Treasury. Even the very rich people, of whom there were about thirty in the town, people who would lose a whole estate at cards, used to drink the bad water and talk passionately about the loan—and I could never under-stand this, for it seemed to me it would be simpler for them to pay up the two hundred thousand.

I did not know a single honest man in the whole town. My father took bribes, and imagined they were given to him out of respect for his spiritual qualities; the boys at the high school, in order to be promoted, went to lodge with the masters and paid them large sums; the wife of the military commandant took levies from the recruits during the recruiting, and even allowed them to stand her drinks, and once she was so drunk in church that she could not get up from her knees; during the recruiting the doctors also took bribes, and the municipal doctor and the veterinary surgeon levied taxes on the butcher shops and public houses; the district school did a trade in certificates which gave certain privileges in the civil service; the provosts took bribes from the clergy and church-wardens whom they controlled, and on the town council and various committees every one who came before them was pursued with: "One expects thanks!"—and thereby forty copecks had to change hands. And those who did not take bribes, like the High Court officials, were stiff and proud, and shook hands with two fingers, and were distinguished by their indifference and narrow-mindedness. They drank and played cards, married rich women, and always had a bad, insidious influence on those round them. Only the girls had any moral purity; most of them had lofty aspirations and were pure and honest at heart; but they knew nothing of life, and believed that bribes were given to honour spiritual qualities; and when they married, they soon grew old and weak, and were hopelessly lost in the mire of that vulgar, bourgeois existence.

III

A railway was being built in our district. On holidays and thereabouts the town was filled with crowds of ragamuffins called "railies," of whom the people were afraid. I used often to see a miserable wretch with a bloody face, and without a hat, being dragged off by the police, and behind him was the proof of his crime, a samovar or some wet, newly washed linen. The "railies" used to collect near the public houses and on the squares; and they drank, ate, and swore terribly, and whistled after the town prostitutes. To amuse these ruffians our shopkeepers used to make the cats and dogs drink vodka, or tie a kerosene-tin to a dog's tail, and whistle to make the dog come tearing along the street with the tin clattering after him, and making him squeal with terror and think he had some frightful monster hard at his heels, so that he would rush out of the town and over the fields until he could run no more. We had several dogs in the town which were left with a permanent shiver and used to crawl about with their tails between their legs, and people said that they could not stand such tricks and had gone mad.

The station was being built five miles from the town. It was said that the engineer had asked for a bribe of fifty thousand roubles to bring the station nearer, but the municipality would only agree to forty; they would not give in to the extra ten thousand, and now the townspeople are sorry because they had to make a road to the station which cost them more. Sleepers and rails were fixed all along the line, and service-trains were running to carry building materials and labourers, and they were only waiting for the bridges upon which Dolyhikov was at work, and here and there the stations were not ready.

Dubechnia—the name of our first station—was seventeen versts from the town. I went on foot. The winter and spring corn was bright green, shining in the morning sun. The road was smooth and bright, and in the distance I could see in outline the station, the hills, and the remote farmhouses.... How good it was out in the open! And how I longed to be filled with the sense of freedom, if only for that morning, to stop thinking of what was going on in the town, or of my needs, or even of eating! Nothing has so much prevented my living as the feeling of acute hunger, which make my finest thoughts get mixed up with thoughts of porridge, cutlets, and fried fish. When I stand alone in the fields and look up at the larks hanging marvellously in the air, and bursting with hysterical song, I think: "It would be nice to have some bread and butter." Or when I sit in the road and shut my eyes and listen to the wonderful sounds of a May-day, I remember how good hot potatoes smell. Being big and of a strong constitution I never have quite enough to eat, and so my chief sensation during the day is hunger, and so I can understand why so many people who are working for a bare living, can talk of nothing but food.

At Dubechnia the station was being plastered inside, and the upper story of the water-tank was being built. It was close and smelt of lime, and the labourers were wandering lazily over piles of chips and rubbish. The signalman was asleep near his box with the sun pouring straight into his face. There was not a single tree. The telephone gave a faint hum, and here and there birds had alighted on it. I wandered over the heaps, not knowing what to do, and remembered how when I asked the engineer what my duties would be, he had replied: "We will see there." But what was there to see in such a wilderness? The plasterers were talking about the foreman and about one Fedot Vassilievich. I could not understand and was filled with embarrassment—physical embarrassment. I felt conscious of my arms and legs, and of the whole of my big body, and did not know what to do with them or where to go.

After walking for at least a couple of hours I noticed that from the station to the right of the line there were telegraph-poles which after about one and a half or two miles ended in a white stone wall. The labourers said it was the office, and I decided at last that I must go there.

It was a very old farmhouse, long unused. The wall of rough, white stone was decayed, and in places had crumbled away, and the roof of the wing, the blind wall of which looked toward the railway, had perished, and was patched here and there with tin.

Through the gates there was a large yard, overgrown with tall grass, and beyond that, an old house with Venetian blinds in the windows, and a high roof, brown with rot. On either side of the house, to right and left, were two symmetrical wings; the windows of one were boarded up, while by the other, the windows of which were open, there were a number of calves grazing. The last telegraph-pole stood in the yard, and the wire went from it to the wing with the blind wall. The door was open and I went in. By the table at the telegraph was sitting a man with a dark, curly head in a canvas coat; he glared at me sternly and askance, but he immediately smiled and said:

"How do you do, Profit?"

It was Ivan Cheprakov, my school friend, who was expelled, when he was in the second class, for smoking. Once, during the autumn, we were out catching goldfinches, starlings, and hawfinches, to sell them in the market early in the morning when our parents were still asleep.

We beat up flocks of starlings and shot at them with pellets, and then picked up the wounded, and some died in terrible agony—I can still remember how they moaned at night in my case—and some recovered. And we sold them, and swore black and blue that they were male birds. Once in the market I had only one starling left, which I hawked about and finally sold for a copeck. "A little profit!" I said to console myself, and from that time at school I was always known as "Little Profit," and even now, schoolboys and the townspeople sometimes use the name to tease me, though no one but myself remembers how it came about.

Cheprakov never was strong. He was narrow-chested, round-shouldered, long-legged. His tie looked like a piece of string, he had no waistcoat, and his boots were worse than mine—with the heels worn down. He blinked with his eyes and had an eager expression as though he were trying to catch something and he was in a constant fidget.

"You wait," he said, bustling about. "Look here!... What was I saying just now?"

We began to talk. I discovered that the estate had till recently belonged to the Cheprakovs and only the previous autumn had passed to Dolyhikov, who thought it more profitable to keep his money in land than in shares, and had already bought three big estates in our district with the transfer of all mortgages. When Cheprakov's mother sold, she stipulated for the right to live in one of the wings for another two years and got her son a job in the office.

"Why shouldn't he buy?" said Cheprakov of the engineer. "He gets a lot from the contractors. He bribes them all."

Then he took me to dinner, deciding in his emphatic way that I was to live with him in the wing and board with his mother.

"She is a screw," he said, "but she will not take much from you."

In the small rooms where his mother lived there was a queer jumble; even the hall and the passage were stacked with furniture, which had been taken from the house after the sale of the estate; and the furniture was old, and of redwood. Mrs. Cheprakov, a very stout elderly lady, with slanting, Chinese eyes, sat by the window, in a big chair, knitting a stocking. She received me ceremoniously.

"It is Pologniev, mother," said Cheprakov, introducing me. "He is going to work here."

"Are you a nobleman?" she asked in a strange, unpleasant voice as though she had boiling fat in her throat.

"Yes," I answered.

"Sit down."

The dinner was bad. It consisted only of a pie with unsweetened curds and some milk soup. Elena Nikifirovna, my hostess, was perpetually winking, first with one eye, then with the other. She talked and ate, but in her whole aspect there was a deathlike quality, and one could almost detect the smell of a corpse. Life hardly stirred in her, yet she had the air of being the lady of the manor, who had once had her serfs, and was the wife of a general, whose servants had to call him "Your Excellency," and when these miserable embers of life flared up in her for a moment, she would say to her son:

"Ivan, that is not the way to hold your knife!"

Or she would say, gasping for breath, with the preciseness of a hostess labouring to entertain her guest:

"We have just sold our estate, you know. It is a pity, of course, we have got so used to being here, but Dolyhikov promised to make Ivan station-master at Dubechnia, so that we shan't have to leave. We shall live here on the station, which is the same as living on the estate. The engineer is such a nice man! Don't you think him very handsome?"

Until recently the Cheprakovs had been very well-to-do, but with the general's death everything changed. Elena Nikifirovna began to quarrel with the neighbours and to go to law, and she did not pay her bailiffs and labourers; she was always afraid of being robbed—and in less than ten years Dubechnia changed completely.

Behind the house there was an old garden run wild, overgrown with tall grass and brushwood. I walked along the terrace which was still well-kept and beautiful; through the glass door I saw a room with a parquet floor, which must have been the draw-ing-room. It contained an ancient piano, some engravings in ma-hogany frames on the walls—and nothing else. There was noth-ing left of the flower-garden but peonies and poppies, rearing their white and scarlet heads above the ground; on the paths, all huddled together, were young maples and elm-trees, which had been stripped by the cows. The growth was dense and the gar-den seemed impassable, and only near the house, where there still stood poplars, firs, and some old bricks, were there traces of the former avenues, and further on the garden was being cleared for a hay-field, and here it was no longer allowed to run wild, and one's mouth and eyes were no longer filled with spiders' webs, and a pleasant air was stirring. The further out one went, the more open it was, and there were cherry-trees, plum-trees, wide-spreading old apple-trees, lichened and held up with props, and the pear-trees were so tall that it was incredible that there could be pears on them. This part of the garden was let to the market-women of our town, and it was guarded from thieves and starlings by a peasant—an idiot who lived in a hut.

The orchard grew thinner and became a mere meadow running down to the river, which was overgrown with reeds and withy-beds. There was a pool by the mill-dam, deep and full of fish, and a little mill with a straw roof ground and roared, and the frogs croaked furiously. On the water, which was as smooth as glass, circles appeared from time to time, and water-lilies trembled on the impact of a darting fish. The village of Dubechnia was on the other side of the river. The calm, azure pool was alluring with its promise of coolness and rest. And now all this, the pool, the mill, the comfortable banks of the river, belonged to the engineer!

And here my new work began. I received and despatched tel-egrams, I wrote out various accounts and copied orders, claims, and reports, sent in to the office by our illiterate foremen and me-chanics. But most of the day I did nothing, walking up and down the room waiting for telegrams, or I would tell the boy to stay in the wing, and go into the garden until the boy came to say the bell was ringing. I had dinner with Mrs. Cheprakov. Meat was served very rarely; most of the dishes were made of milk, and on Wednesdays and Fridays we had Lenten fare, and the food was served in pink plates, which were called Lenten. Mrs. Cheprakov was always blinking—the habit grew on her, and I felt awkward and embarrassed in her presence.

As there was not enough work for one, Cheprakov did nothing, but slept or went down to the pool with his gun to shoot ducks. In the evenings he got drunk in the village, or at the station, and before going to bed he would look in the glass and say:

"How are you, Ivan Cheprakov?"

When he was drunk, he was very pale and used to rub his hands and laugh, or rather neigh, He-he-he! Out of bravado he would undress himself and run naked through the fields, and he used to eat flies and say they were a bit sour.

IV

Once after dinner he came running into the wing, panting, to say:

"Your sister has come to see you."

I went out and saw a fly standing by the steps of the house. My sister had brought Aniuta Blagovo and a military gentleman in a summer uniform. As I approached I recognised the military gentleman as Aniuta's brother, the doctor.

"We've come to take you for a picnic," he said, "if you've no objection."

My sister and Aniuta wanted to ask how I was getting on, but they were both silent and only looked at me. They felt that I didn't like my job, and tears came into my sister's eyes and Aniuta Blagovo blushed. We went into the orchard, the doctor first, and he said ecstatically:

"What air! By Jove, what air!"

He was just a boy to look at. He talked and walked like an undergraduate, and the look in his grey eyes was as lively, simple, and frank as that of a nice boy. Compared with his tall, handsome sister he looked weak and slight, and his little beard was thin and so was his voice—a thin tenor, though quite pleasant. He was away somewhere with his regiment and had come home on leave, and said that he was going to Petersburg in the autumn to take his M.D. He already had a family—a wife and three children; he had married young, in his second year at the University, and people said he was unhappily married and was not living with his wife.

"What is the time?" My sister was uneasy. "We must go back soon, for my father would only let me have until six o'clock."

"Oh, your father," sighed the doctor.

I made tea, and we drank it sitting on a carpet in front of the terrace, and the doctor, kneeling, drank from his saucer, and said that he was perfectly happy. Then Cheprakov fetched the key and unlocked the glass door and we all entered the house. It was dark and mysterious and smelled of mushrooms, and our footsteps made a hollow sound as though there were a vault under the floor. The doctor stopped by the piano and touched the keys and it gave out a faint, tremulous, cracked but still melodious sound. He raised his voice and began to sing a romance, frowning and impatiently stamping his foot when he touched a broken key. My sister forgot about going home, but walked agitatedly up and down the room and said:

"I am happy! I am very, very happy!"

There was a note of surprise in her voice as though it seemed impossible to her that she should be happy. It was the first time in my life that I had seen her so gay. She even looked handsome. Her profile was not good, her nose and mouth somehow protruded and made her look as if she was always blowing, but she had beautiful, dark eyes, a pale, very delicate complexion, and a touching expression of kindness and sadness, and when she spoke she seemed very charming and even beautiful. Both she and I took after our mother; we were broad-shouldered, strong, and sturdy, but her paleness was a sign of sickness, she often coughed, and in her eyes I often noticed the expression common to people who are ill, but who for some reason conceal it. In her present cheerfulness there was something childish and naïve, as though all the joy which had been suppressed and dulled during our childhood by a strict upbringing, had suddenly awakened in her soul and rushed out into freedom.

But when evening came and the fly was brought round, my sister became very quiet and subdued, and sat in the fly as though it were a prison-van.

Soon they were all gone. The noise of the fly died away.... I remembered that Aniuta Blagovo had said not a single word to me all day.

"A wonderful girl!" I thought "A wonderful girl."

Lent came and every day we had Lenten dishes. I was greatly depressed by my idleness and the uncertainty of my position, and, slothful, hungry, dissatisfied with myself, I wandered over the estate and only waited for an energetic mood to leave the place.

Once in the afternoon when Radish was sitting in our wing, Dolyhikov entered unexpectedly, very sunburnt, and grey with dust. He had been out on the line for three days and had come to Dubechnia on a locomotive and walked over. While he waited for the carriage which he had ordered to come out to meet him he went over the estate with his bailiff, giving orders in a loud voice, and then for a whole hour he sat in our wing and wrote letters. When telegrams came through for him, he himself tapped out the answers, while we stood there stiff and silent.

"What a mess!" he said, looking angrily through the accounts. "I shall transfer the office to the station in a fortnight and I don't know what I shall do with you then."

"I've done my best, sir," said Cheprakov.

"Quite so. I can see what your best is. You can only draw your wages." The engineer looked at me and went on. "You rely on getting introductions to make a career for yourself with as little trouble as possible. Well, I don't care about introductions. Nobody helped me. Before I had this line, I was an engine-driver. I worked in Belgium as an ordinary lubricator. And what are you doing here, Panteley?" he asked, turning to Radish. "Going out drinking?"

For some reason or other he called all simple people Panteley, while he despised men like Cheprakov and myself, and called us drunkards, beasts, canaille. As a rule he was hard on petty officials, and paid and dismissed them ruthlessly without any explanation.

At last the carriage came for him. When he left he promised to dismiss us all in a fortnight; called the bailiff a fool, stretched himself out comfortably in the carriage, and drove away.

"Andrey Ivanich," I said to Radish, "will you take me on as a labourer?"

"What! Why?"

We went together toward the town, and when the station and the farm were far behind us, I asked:

"Andrey Ivanich, why did you come to Dubechnia?"

"Firstly because some of my men are working on the line, and secondly to pay interest to Mrs. Cheprakov. I borrowed fifty roubles from her last summer, and now I pay her one rouble a month."

The decorator stopped and took hold of my coat.

"Misail Alereich, my friend," he went on, "I take it that if a common man or a gentleman takes interest, he is a wrong-doer. The truth is not in him."

Radish, looking thin, pale, and rather terrible, shut his eyes, shook his head, and muttered in a philosophic tone:

"The grub eats grass, rust eats iron, lies devour the soul. God save us miserable sinners!"

91

V

Radish was unpractical and he was no business man; he undertook more work than he could do, and when he came to payment he always lost his reckoning and so was always out on the wrong side. He was a painter, a glazier, a paper-hanger, and would even take on tiling, and I remember how he used to run about for days looking for tiles to make an insignificant profit. He was an excellent workman and would sometimes earn ten roubles a day, and but for his desire to be a master and to call himself a contractor, he would probably have made quite a lot of money.

He himself was paid by contract and paid me and the others by the day, between seventy-five copecks and a rouble per day. When the weather was hot and dry he did various outside jobs, chiefly painting roofs. Not being used to it, my feet got hot, as though I were walking over a red-hot oven, and when I wore felt boots my feet swelled. But this was only at the beginning. Later on I got used to it and everything went all right. I lived among the people, to whom work was obligatory and unavoidable, people who worked like dray-horses, and knew nothing of the moral value of labour, and never even used the word "labour" in their talk. Among them I also felt like a dray-horse, more and more imbued with the necessity and inevitability of what I was doing, and this made my life easier, and saved me from doubt.

At first everything amused me, everything was new. It was like being born again. I could sleep on the ground and go barefoot— and found it exceedingly pleasant. I could stand in a crowd of simple folks, without embarrassing them, and when a cab-horse fell down in the street, I used to run and help it up without being afraid of soiling my clothes. But, best of all, I was living independently and was not a burden on any one.

The painting of roofs, especially when we mixed our own paint, was considered a very profitable business, and, therefore, even such good workmen as Radish did not shun this rough and tiresome work. In short trousers, showing his lean, muscular legs, he used to prowl over the roof like a stork, and I used to hear him sigh wearily as he worked his brush:

"Woe, woe to us, miserable sinners!"

He could walk as easily on a roof as on the ground. In spite of his looking so ill and pale and corpse-like, his agility was extraordinary; like any young man he would paint the cupola and the top of the church without scaffolding, using only ladders and a rope, and it was queer and strange when, standing there, far above the ground, he would rise to his full height and cry to the world at large:

"Grubs eat grass, rust eats iron, lies devour the soul!"

Or, thinking of something, he would suddenly answer his own thought:

"Anything may happen! Anything may happen!"

When I went home from work all the people sitting outside their doors, the shop assistants, dogs, and their masters, used to shout after me and jeer spitefully, and at first it seemed monstrous and distressed me greatly.

"Little Profit," they used to shout. "House-painter! Yellow ochre!"

And no one treated me so unmercifully as those who had only just risen above the people and had quite recently had to work for their living. Once in the market-place as I passed the ironmonger's a can of water was spilled over me as if by accident, and once a stick was thrown at me. And once a fishmonger, a grey-haired old man, stood in my way and looked at me morosely and said:

"It isn't you I'm sorry for, you fool, it's your father."

And when my acquaintances met me they got confused. Some regarded me as a queer fish and a fool, and they were sorry for me; others did not know how to treat me and it was difficult to understand them. Once, in the daytime, in one of the streets off Great Gentry Street, I met Aniuta Blagovo. I was on my way to my work and was carrying two long brushes and a pot of paint. When she recognised me, Aniuta blushed.

"Please do not acknowledge me in the street," she said nervously, sternly, in a trembling voice, without offering to shake hands with me, and tears suddenly gleamed in her eyes. "If you must be like this, then, so—so be it, but please avoid me in public!"

I had left Great Gentry Street and was living in a suburb called Makarikha with my nurse Karpovna, a good-natured but gloomy old woman who was always looking for evil, and was frightened by her dreams, and saw omens and ill in the bees and wasps which flew into her room. And in her opinion my having become a working man boded no good.

"You are lost!" she said mournfully, shaking her head. "Lost!"

With her in her little house lived her adopted son, Prokofyi, a butcher, a huge, clumsy fellow, of about thirty, with ginger hair and scrubby moustache. When he met me in the hall, he would silently and respectfully make way for me, and when he was drunk he would salute me with his whole hand. In the evenings he used to have supper, and through the wooden partition I could hear him snorting and snuffling as he drank glass after glass.

"Mother," he would say in an undertone.

"Well," Karpovna would reply. She was passionately fond of him. "What is it, my son?"

"I'll do you a favour, mother. I'll feed you in your old age in this vale of tears, and when you die I'll bury you at my own expense. So I say and so I'll do."

I used to get up every day before sunrise and go to bed early. We painters ate heavily and slept soundly, and only during the night would we have any excitement. I never quarrelled with my comrades. All day long there was a ceaseless stream of abuse, cursing and hearty good wishes, as, for instance, that one's eyes should burst, or that one might be carried off by cholera, but, all the same, among ourselves we were very friendly. The men suspected me of being a religious crank and used to laugh at me good-naturedly, saying that even my own father denounced me, and they used to say that they very seldom went to church and that many of them had not been to confession for ten years, and they justified their laxness by saying that a decorator is among men like a jackdaw among birds.

My mates respected me and regarded me with esteem; they evidently liked my not drinking or smoking, and leading a quiet, steady life. They were only rather disagreeably surprised at my not stealing the oil, or going with them to ask our employers for a drink. The stealing of the employers' oil and paint was a custom with house-painters, and was not regarded as theft, and it was remarkable that even so honest a man as Radish would always come away from work with some white lead and oil. And even respectable old men who had their own houses in Makarikha were not ashamed to ask for tips, and when the men, at the beginning or end of a job, made up to some vulgar fool and thanked him humbly for a few pence, I used to feel sick and sorry.

With the customers they behaved like sly courtiers, and almost every day I was reminded of Shakespeare's Polonius.

"There will probably be rain," a customer would say, staring at the sky.

"It is sure to rain," the painters would agree.

"But the clouds aren't rain-clouds. Perhaps it won't rain."

"No, sir. It won't rain. It won't rain, sure."

Behind their backs they generally regarded the customers ironically, and when, for instance, they saw a gentleman sitting on his balcony with a newspaper, they would say:

"He reads newspapers, but he has nothing to eat."

I never visited my people. When I returned from work I often found short, disturbing notes from my sister about my father; how he was very absent-minded at dinner, and then slipped away and locked himself in his study and did not come out for a long time. Such news upset me. I could not sleep, and I would go sometimes at night and walk along Great Gentry Street by our house, and look up at the dark windows, and try to guess if all was well within. On Sundays my sister would come to see me, but by stealth, as though she came not to see me, but my nurse. And if she came into my room she would look pale, with her eyes red, and at once she would begin to weep.

"Father cannot bear it much longer," she would say. "If, as God forbid, something were to happen to him, it would be on your conscience all your life. It is awful, Misail! For mother's sake I implore you to mend your ways."

"My dear sister," I replied. "How can I reform when I am convinced that I am acting according to my conscience? Do try to understand me!"

"I know you are obeying your conscience, but it ought to be possible to do so without hurting anybody."

"Oh, saints above!" the old woman would sigh behind the door. "You are lost. There will be a misfortune, my dear. It is bound to come."

VI

On Sunday, Doctor Blagovo came to see me unexpectedly. He was wearing a white summer uniform over a silk shirt, and high glacé boots.

"I came to see you!" he began, gripping my hand in his hearty, undergraduate fashion. "I hear of you every day and I have long intended to go and see you to have a heart-to-heart, as they say. Things are awfully boring in the town; there is not a living soul worth talking to. How hot it is, by Jove!" he went on, taking off his tunic and standing in his silk shirt. "My dear fellow, let us have a talk."

I was feeling bored and longing for other society than that of the decorators. I was really glad to see him.

"To begin with," he said, sitting on my bed, "I sympathise with you heartily, and I have a profound respect for your present way of living. In the town you are misunderstood and there is nobody to understand you, because, as you know, it is full of Gogolian pig-faces. But I guessed what you were at the picnic. You are a noble soul, an honest, high-minded man! I respect you and think it an honour to shake hands with you. To change your life so abruptly and suddenly as you did, you must have passed through a most trying spiritual process, and to go on with it now, to live scrupulously by your convictions, you must have to toil incessantly both in mind and in heart. Now, please tell me, don't you think that if you spent all this force of will, intensity, and power on something else, like trying to be a great scholar or an artist, that your life would be both wider and deeper, and altogether more productive?"

We talked and when we came to speak of physical labour, I expressed this idea: that it was necessary that the strong should not enslave the weak, and that the minority should not be a parasite on the majority, always sucking up the finest sap, i. e., it was necessary that all without exception—the strong and the weak, the rich and the poor—should share equally in the struggle for existence, every man for himself, and in that respect there was no better means of levelling than physical labour and compulsory service for all.

"You think, then," said the doctor, "that all, without, exception, should be employed in physical labour?"

"Yes."

"But don't you think that if everybody, including the best people, thinkers and men of science, were to take part in the struggle for existence, each man for himself, and took to breaking stones and painting roofs, it would be a serious menace to progress?"

"Where is the danger?" I asked. "Progress consists in deeds of love, in the fulfilment of the moral law. If you enslave no one, and are a burden upon no one, what further progress do you want?"

"But look here!" said Blagovo, suddenly losing his temper and getting up. "I say! If a snail in its shell is engaged in self-perfection in obedience to the moral law—would you call that progress?"

"But why?" I was nettled. "If you make your neighbours feed you, clothe you, carry you, defend you from your enemies, their life is built up on slavery, and that is not progress. My view is that that is the most real and, perhaps, the only possible, the only progress necessary."

"The limits of universal progress, which is common to all men, are in infinity, and it seems to me strange to talk of a 'possible' progress limited by our needs and temporal conceptions."

"If the limits of peoples are in infinity, as you say, then it means that its goal is indefinite," I said. "Think of living without knowing definitely what for!"

"Why not? Your 'not knowing' is not so boring as your 'knowing.' I am walking up a ladder which is called progress, civilisation, culture. I go on and on, not knowing definitely where I am going to, but surely it is worth while living for the sake of the wonderful ladder alone. And you know exactly what you are living for—that some should not enslave others, that the artist and the man who mixes his colours for him should dine together. But that is the bourgeois, kitchen side of life, and isn't it disgusting only to live for that? If some insects devour others, devil take them, let them! We need not think of them, they will perish and rot, however you save them from slavery—we must think of that great Cross which awaits all mankind in the distant future."

Blagovo argued hotly with me, but it was noticeable that he was disturbed by some outside thought.

"Your sister is not coming," he said, consulting his watch. "Yesterday she was at our house and said she was going to see you. You go on talking about slavery, slavery," he went on, "but it is a special question, and all these questions are solved by mankind gradually."

We began to talk of evolution. I said that every man decides the question of good and evil for himself, and does not wait for mankind to solve the question by virtue of gradual development. Besides, evolution is a stick with two ends. Side by side with the gradual development of humanitarian ideas, there is the gradual growth of ideas of a different kind. Serfdom is past, and capitalism is growing. And with ideas of liberation at their height the majority, just as in the days of Baty, feeds, clothes, and defends the minority; and is left hungry, naked, and defenceless. The state of things harmonises beautifully with all your tendencies and movements, because the art of enslaving is also being gradually developed. We no longer flog our servants in the stables, but we give slavery more refined forms; at any rate, we are able to justify it in each separate case. Ideas remain ideas with us, but if we could, now, at the end of the nineteenth century, throw upon the working classes all our most unpleasant physiological functions, we should do so, and, of course, we should justify ourselves by saying that if the best people, thinkers and great scholars, had to waste their time on such functions, progress would be in serious jeopardy.

Just then my sister entered. When she saw the doctor, she was flurried and excited, and at once began to say that it was time for her to go home to her father.

"Cleopatra Alexeyevna," said Blagovo earnestly, laying his hands on his heart, "what will happen to your father if you spend half an hour with your brother and me?"

He was a simple kind of man and could communicate his cheerfulness to others. My sister thought for a minute and began to laugh, and suddenly got very happy, suddenly, unexpectedly, just as she did at the picnic. We went out into the fields and lay on the grass, and went on with our conversation and looked at the town, where all the windows facing the west looked golden in the setting sun.

After that Blagovo appeared every time my sister came to see me, and they always greeted each other as though their meeting was unexpected. My sister used to listen while the doctor and I argued, and her face was always joyful and rapturous, admiring and curious, and it seemed to me that a new world was slowly being discovered before her eyes, a world which she had not seen before even in her dreams, which now she was trying to divine; when the doctor was not there she was quiet and sad, and if, as she sat on my bed, she sometimes wept, it was for reasons of which she did not speak.

In August Radish gave us orders to go to the railway. A couple of days before we were "driven" out of town, my father came to see me. He sat down and, without looking at me, slowly wiped his red face, then took out of his pocket our local paper and read out with deliberate emphasis on each word that a schoolfellow of my own age, the son of the director of the State Bank, had been appointed chief clerk of the Court of the Exchequer.

"And now, look at yourself," he said, folding up the newspaper. "You are a beggar, a vagabond, a scoundrel! Even the bourgeoisie and other peasants get education to make themselves decent people, while you, a Pologniev, with famous, noble ancestors, go wallowing in the mire! But I did not come here to talk to you. I have given you up already." He went on in a choking voice, as he stood up: "I came here to find out where your sister is, you scoundrel! She left me after dinner. It is now past seven o'clock and she is not in. She has been going out lately without telling me, and she has been disrespectful—and I see your filthy, abominable influence at work. Where is she?"

He had in his hands the familiar umbrella, and I was already taken aback, and I stood stiff and erect, like a schoolboy, waiting for my father to thrash me, but he saw the glance I cast at the umbrella and this probably checked him.

"Live as you like!" he said. "My blessing is gone from you."

"Good God!" muttered my old nurse behind the door. "You are lost. Oh! my heart feels some misfortune coming. I can feel it."

I went to work on the railway. During the whole of August there

was wind and rain. It was damp and cold; the corn had now been
gathered in the fields, and on the big farms where the reaping was
done with machines, the wheat lay not in stacks, but in heaps; and
I remember how those melancholy heaps grew darker and darker
every day, and the grain sprouted. It was hard work; the pouring
rain spoiled everything that we succeeded in finishing. We were
not allowed either to live or to sleep in the station buildings and
had to take shelter in dirty, damp, mud huts where the "railies"
had lived during the summer, and at night I could not sleep from
the cold and the bugs crawling over my face and hands. And
when we were working near the bridges, then the "railies" used to
come out in a crowd to fight the painters—which they regarded as
sport. They used to thrash us, steal our trousers, and to infuriate
us and provoke us to a fight; they used to spoil our work, as when
they smeared the signal-boxes with green paint. To add to all our
miseries Radish began to pay us very irregularly. All the painting
on the line was given to one contractor, who subcontracted with
another, and he again with Radish, stipulating for twenty per cent
commission. The job itself was unprofitable; then came the rains;
time was wasted; we did no work and Radish had to pay his men
every day. The starving painters nearly came to blows with him,
called him a swindler, a bloodsucker, a Judas, and he, poor man,
sighed and in despair raised his hands to the heavens and was
continually going to Mrs. Cheprakov to borrow money.

VII

Came the rainy, muddy, dark autumn, bringing a slack time,
and I used to sit at home three days in the week without work,
or did various jobs outside painting; such as digging earth for
ballast for twenty copecks a day. Doctor Blagovo had gone to Petersburg. My sister did not come to see me. Radish lay at home ill,
expecting to die every day.

And my mood was also autumnal; perhaps because when I became a working man I saw only the seamy side of the life of our
town, and every day made fresh discoveries which brought me
to despair. My fellow townsmen, both those of whom I had had a
low opinion before, and those whom I had thought fairly decent,
now seemed to me base, cruel, and up to any dirty trick. We poor
people were tricked and cheated in the accounts, kept waiting for
hours in cold passages or in the kitchen, and we were insulted
and uncivilly treated. In the autumn I had to paper the library
and two rooms at the club. I was paid seven copecks a piece, but
was told to give a receipt for twelve copecks, and when I refused

to do it, a respectable gentleman in gold spectacles, one of the stewards of the club, said to me:

"If you say another word, you scoundrel, I'll knock you down."

And when a servant whispered to him that I was the son of Pologniev, the architect, then I got flustered and blushed, but he recovered himself at once and said:

"Damn him."

In the shops we working men were sold bad meat, musty flour, and coarse tea. In church we were jostled by the police, and in the hospitals we were mulcted by the assistants and nurses, and if we could not give them bribes through poverty, we were given food in dirty dishes. In the post-office the lowest official considered it his duty to treat us as animals and to shout rudely and insolently: "Wait! Don't you come pushing your way in here!" Even the dogs, even they were hostile to us and hurled themselves at us with a peculiar malignancy. But what struck me most of all in my new position was the entire lack of justice, what the people call "forgetting God." Rarely a day went by without some swindle. The shopkeeper, who sold us oil, the contractor, the workmen, the customers themselves, all cheated. It was an understood thing that our rights were never considered, and we always had to pay for the money we had earned, going with our hats off to the back door.

I was paper-hanging in one of the club-rooms, next the library, when, one evening as I was on the point of leaving, Dolyhikov's daughter came into the room carrying a bundle of books.

I bowed to her.

"Ah! How are you?" she said, recognising me at once and holding out her hand. "I am very glad to see you."

She smiled and looked with a curious puzzled expression at my blouse and the pail of paste and the papers lying on the floor; I was embarrassed and she also felt awkward.

"Excuse my staring at you," she said. "I have heard so much about you. Especially from Doctor Blagovo. He is enthusiastic about you. I have met your sister; she is a dear, sympathetic girl, but I could not make her see that there is nothing awful in your simple life. On the contrary, you are the most interesting man in the town."

Once more she glanced at the pail of paste and the paper and said:

"I asked Doctor Blagovo to bring us together, but he either forgot or had no time. However, we have met now. I should be very pleased if you would call on me. I do so want to have a talk. I am a simple person," she said, holding out her hand, "and I hope you will come and see me without ceremony. My father is away, in Petersburg."

She went into the reading-room, with her dress rustling, and for a long time after I got home I could not sleep.

During that autumn some kind soul, wishing to relieve my existence, sent me from time to time presents of tea and lemons, or biscuits, or roast pigeons. Karpovna said the presents were brought by a soldier, though from whom she did not know; and the soldier used to ask if I was well, if I had dinner every day, and if I had warm clothes. When the frost began the soldier came while I was out and brought a soft knitted scarf, which gave out a soft, hardly perceptible scent, and I guessed who my good fairy had been. For the scarf smelled of lily-of-the-valley, Aniuta Blagovo's favourite scent.

Toward winter there was more work and things became more cheerful. Radish came to life again and we worked together in the cemetery church, where we scraped the holy shrine for gilding. It was a clean, quiet, and, as our mates said, a specially good job. We could do a great deal in one day, and so time passed quickly, imperceptibly. There was no swearing, nor laughing, nor loud altercations. The place compelled quiet and decency, and disposed one for tranquil, serious thoughts. Absorbed in our work, we stood or sat immovably, like statues; there was a dead silence, very proper to a cemetery, so that if a tool fell down, or the oil in the lamp spluttered, the sound would be loud and startling, and we would turn to see what it was. After a long silence one could hear a humming like that of a swarm of bees; in the porch, in an undertone, the funeral service was being read over a dead baby; or a painter painting a moon surrounded with stars on the cupola would begin to whistle quietly, and remembering suddenly that he was in a church, would stop; or Radish would sigh at his own thoughts: "Anything may happen! Anything may happen!" or above our heads there would be the slow, mournful tolling of a bell, and the painters would say it must be a rich man being brought to the church....

The days I spent in the peace of the little church, and during the evenings I played billiards, or went to the gallery of the theatre in the new serge suit I had bought with my own hard-earned money. They were already beginning plays and concerts at the Azhoguins', and Radish did the scenery by himself. He told me about the plays and tableaux vivants at the Azhoguins', and I listened to him enviously. I had a great longing to take part in the rehearsals, but I dared not go to the Azhoguins'.

A week before Christmas Doctor Blagovo arrived, and we resumed our arguments and played billiards in the evenings. When he played billiards he used to take off his coat, and unfasten his shirt at the neck, and generally try to look like a debauchee. He drank a little, but rowdily, and managed to spend in a cheap tavern like the Volga as much as twenty roubles in an evening.

Once more my sister came to see me, and when they met they expressed surprise, but I could see by her happy, guilty face that these meetings were not accidental. One evening when we were playing billiards the doctor said to me:

"I say, why don't you call on Miss Dolyhikov? You don't know Maria Victorovna. She is a clever, charming, simple creature."

I told him how the engineer had received me in the spring.

"Nonsense!" laughed the doctor. "The engineer is one thing and she is another. Really, my good fellow, you mustn't offend her. Go and see her some time. Let us go to-morrow evening. Will you?"

He persuaded me. Next evening I donned my serge suit and with some perturbation set out to call on Miss Dolyhikov. The footman did not seem to me so haughty and formidable, or the furniture so oppressive, as on the morning when I had come to ask for work. Maria Victorovna was expecting me and greeted me as an old friend and gave my hand a warm, friendly grip. She was wearing a grey dress with wide sleeves, and had her hair done in the style which when it became the fashion a year later in our town, was called "dog's ears." The hair was combed back over the ears, and it made Maria Victorovna's face look broader, and she looked very like her father, whose face was broad and red and rather like a coachman's. She was handsome and elegant, but not young; about thirty to judge by her appearance, though she was not more than twenty-five.

"Dear doctor!" she said, making me sit down. "How grateful I am to him. But for him, you would not have come. I am bored to death! My father has gone and left me alone, and I do not know what to do with myself."

Then she began to ask where I was working, how much I got, and where I lived.

"Do you only spend what you earn on yourself?" she asked.

"Yes."

"You are a happy man," she replied. "All the evil in life, it seems to me, comes from boredom and idleness, and spiritual emptiness, which are inevitable when one lives at other people's expense. Don't think I'm showing off. I mean it sincerely. It is dull and unpleasant to be rich. Win friends by just riches, they say, because as a rule there is and can be no such thing as just riches."

She looked at the furniture with a serious, cold expression, as though she was making an inventory of it, and went on:

"Ease and comfort possess a magic power. Little by little they seduce even strong-willed people. Father and I used to live poorly and simply, and now you see how we live. Isn't it strange?" she said with a shrug. "We spend twenty thousand roubles a year! In the provinces!"

"Ease and comfort must not be regarded as the inevitable privilege of capital and education," I said. "It seems to me possible to unite the comforts of life with work, however hard and dirty it may be. Your father is rich, but, as he says, he used to be a mechanic, and just a lubricator."

She smiled and shook her head thoughtfully.

"Papa sometimes eats tiurya," she said, "but only out of caprice."

A bell rang and she got up.

"The rich and the educated ought to work like the rest," she went on, "and if there is to be any comfort, it should be accessible to all. There should be no privileges. However, that's enough philosophy. Tell me something cheerful. Tell me about the painters. What are they like? Funny?"

The doctor came. I began to talk about the painters, but, being unused to it, I felt awkward and talked solemnly and ponderously like an ethnographist. The doctor also told a few stories about working people. He rocked to and fro and cried, and fell on his knees, and when he was depicting a drunkard, lay flat on the floor. It was as good as a play, and Maria Victorovna laughed until she cried. Then he played the piano and sang in his high-pitched tenor, and Maria Victorovna stood by him and told him what to sing and corrected him when he made a mistake.

"I hear you sing, too," said I.

"Too?" cried the doctor. "She is a wonderful singer, an artist, and you say—too! Careful, careful!"

"I used to study seriously," she replied, "but I have given it up now."

She sat on a low stool and told us about her life in Petersburg, and imitated famous singers, mimicking their voices and mannerisms; then she sketched the doctor and myself in her album, not very well, but both were good likenesses. She laughed and made jokes and funny faces, and this suited her better than talking about unjust riches, and it seemed to me that what she had said about "riches and comfort" came not from herself, but was just mimicry. She was an admirable comedian. I compared her mentally with the girls of our town, and not even the beautiful, serious Aniuta Blagovo could stand up against her; the difference was as vast as that between a wild and a garden rose.

We stayed to supper. The doctor and Maria Victorovna drank red wine, champagne, and coffee with cognac; they touched glasses and drank to friendship, to wit, to progress, to freedom, and never got drunk, but went rather red and laughed for no reason until they cried. To avoid being out of it I, too, drank red wine.

"People with talent and with gifted natures," said Miss Dolyhikov, "know how to live and go their own way; but ordinary people like myself know nothing and can do nothing by themselves; there is nothing for them but to find some deep social current and let themselves be borne along by it."

"Is it possible to find that which does not exist?" asked the doctor.

"It doesn't exist because we don't see it."

"Is that so? Social currents are the invention of modern literature. They don't exist here."

A discussion began.

"We have no profound social movements; nor have we had them," said the doctor. "Modern literature has invented a lot of things, and modern literature invented intellectual working men in village life, but go through all our villages and you will only find Mr. Cheeky Snout in a jacket or black frock coat, who will make four mistakes in the word 'one.' Civilised life has not begun with us yet. We have the same savagery, the same slavery, the same nullity as we had five hundred years ago. Movements, currents—all that is so wretched and puerile mixed up with such vulgar, catch-penny interests—and one cannot take it seriously. You may think you have discovered a large social movement, and you may follow it and devote your life in the modern fashion to such problems as the liberation of vermin from slavery, or the abolition of meat cutlets—and I congratulate you, madam. But we have to learn, learn, learn, and there will be plenty of time for social movements; we are not up to them yet, and upon my soul, we don't understand anything at all about them."

"You don't understand, but I do," said Maria Victorovna. "Good Heavens! What a bore you are to-night."

"It is our business to learn and learn, to try and accumulate as much knowledge as possible, because serious social movements come where there is knowledge, and the future happiness of mankind lies in science. Here's to science!"

"One thing is certain. Life must somehow be arranged different-ly," said Maria Victorovna, after some silence and deep thought, "and life as it has been up to now is worthless. Don't let us talk about it."

When we left her the Cathedral clock struck two.

"Did you like her?" asked the doctor. "Isn't she a dear girl?"

We had dinner at Maria Victorovna's on Christmas Day, and then we went to see her every day during the holidays. There was nobody besides ourselves, and she was right when she said she had no friends in the town but the doctor and me. We spent most of the time talking, and sometimes the doctor would bring a book or a magazine and read aloud. After all, he was the first cultivated man I had met. I could not tell if he knew much, but he was always generous with his knowledge because he wished others to know too. When he talked about medicine, he was not like any of our local doctors, but he made a new and singular impression, and it seemed to me that if he had wished he could have become a genuine scientist. And perhaps he was the only person at that time who had any real influence over me. Meeting him and reading the books he gave me, I began gradually to feel a need for knowledge to inspire the tedium of my work. It seemed strange to me that I had not known before such things as that the whole world consisted of sixty elements. I did not know what oil or paint was, and I could do without knowing. My acquaintance with the doctor raised me morally too. I used to argue with him, and though I usually stuck to my opinion, yet, through him, I came gradually to perceive that everything was not clear to me, and I tried to cultivate convictions as definite as possible so that the promptings of my conscience should be precise and have nothing vague about them. Nevertheless, educated and fine as he was, far and away the best man in the town, he was by no means perfect. There was something rather rude and priggish in his ways and in his trick of dragging talk down to discussion, and when he took off his coat and sat in his shirt and gave the footman a tip, it always seemed to me that culture was just a part of him, with the rest untamed Tartar.

After the holidays he left once more for Petersburg. He went in the morning and after dinner my sister came to see me. Without taking off her furs, she sat silent, very pale, staring in front of her. She began to shiver and seemed to be fighting against some illness.

"You must have caught a cold," I said.

Her eyes filled with tears. She rose and went to Karpovna without a word to me, as though I had offended her. And a little later I heard her speaking in a tone of bitter reproach.

"Nurse, what have I been living for, up to now? What for? Tell me; haven't I wasted my youth? During the last years I have had nothing but making up accounts, pouring out tea, counting the copecks, entertaining guests, without a thought that there was anything better in the world! Nurse, try to understand me, I too have human desires and I want to live and they have made a housekeeper of me. It is awful, awful!"

She flung her keys against the door and they fell with a clatter in my room. They were the keys of the side-board, the larder, the cellar, and the tea-chest—the keys my mother used to carry.

"Oh! Oh! Saints above!" cried my old nurse in terror. "The blessed saints!"

When she left, my sister came into my room for her keys and said:

"Forgive me. Something strange has been going on in me lately."

VIII

One evening when I came home late from Maria Victorovna's I found a young policeman in a new uniform in my room; he was sitting by the table reading.

"At last!" he said getting up and stretching himself. "This is the third time I have been to see you. The governor has ordered you to go and see him to-morrow at nine o'clock sharp. Don't be late."

He made me give him a written promise to comply with his Excellency's orders and went away. This policeman's visit and the unexpected invitation to see the governor had a most depressing effect on me. From my early childhood I have had a dread of gendarmes, police, legal officials, and I was tormented with anxiety as though I had really committed a crime and I could not sleep. Nurse and Prokofyi were also upset and could not sleep. And, to make things worse, nurse had an earache, and moaned and more than once screamed out. Hearing that I could not sleep Prokofyi came quietly into my room with a little lamp and sat by the table.

"You should have a drop of pepper-brandy...." he said after some thought. "In this vale of tears things go on all right when you take a drop. And if mother had some pepper-brandy poured into her ear she would be much better."

About three he got ready to go to the slaughter-house to fetch some meat. I knew I should not sleep until morning, and to use up the time until nine, I went with him. We walked with a lantern, and his boy, Nicolka, who was about thirteen, and had blue spots on his face and an expression like a murderer's, drove behind us in a sledge, urging the horse on with hoarse cries.

"You will probably be punished at the governor's," said Prokofyi as we walked. "There is a governor's rank, and an archimandrite's rank, and an officer's rank, and a doctor's rank, and every profession has its own rank. You don't keep to yours and they won't allow it."

The slaughter-house stood behind the cemetery, and till then I had only seen it at a distance. It consisted of three dark sheds surrounded by a grey fence, from which, when the wind was in that direction in summer, there came an overpowering stench. Now, as I entered the yard, I could not see the sheds in the darkness; I groped through horses and sledges, both empty and laden with meat; and there were men walking about with lanterns and swearing disgustingly. Prokofyi and Nicolka swore as filthily and there was a continuous hum from the swearing and coughing and the neighing of the horses.

The place smelled of corpses and offal, the snow was thawing and already mixed with mud, and in the darkness it seemed to me that I was walking through a pool of blood.

When we had filled the sledge with meat, we went to the butcher's shop in the market-place. Day was beginning to dawn. One after another the cooks came with baskets and old women in mantles. With an axe in his hand, wearing a white, blood-stained apron, Prokofyi swore terrifically and crossed himself, turning toward the church, and shouted so loud that he could be heard all over the market, avowing that he sold his meat at cost price and even at a loss. He cheated in weighing and reckoning, the cooks saw it, but, dazed by his shouting, they did not protest, but only called him a gallows-bird.

Raising and dropping his formidable axe, he assumed picturesque attitudes and constantly uttered the sound "Hak!" with a furious expression, and I was really afraid of his cutting off some one's head or hand.

I stayed in the butcher's shop the whole morning, and when at last I went to the governor's my fur coat smelled of meat and blood. My state of mind would have been appropriate for an encounter with a bear armed with no more than a staff. I remember a long staircase with a striped carpet, and a young official in a frock coat with shining buttons, who silently indicated the door with both hands and went in to announce me. I entered the hall, where the furniture was most luxurious, but cold and tasteless, forming a most unpleasant impression—the tall, narrow pier-glasses, and the bright, yellow hangings over the windows; one could see that, though governors changed, the furniture remained the same. The young official again pointed with both hands to the door and went toward a large, green table, by which stood a general with the Order of Vladimir at his neck.

"Mr. Pologniev," he began, holding a letter in his hand and opening his mouth wide so that it made a round O. "I asked you to come to say this to you: 'Your esteemed father has applied verbally and in writing to the provincial marshal of nobility, to have you summoned and made to see the incongruity of your conduct with the title of nobleman which you have the honour to bear. His Excellency Alexander Pavlovich, justly thinking that your conduct may be subversive, and finding that persuasion may not be sufficient, without serious intervention on the part of the authorities, has given me his decision as to your case, and I agree with him.'"

He said this quietly, respectfully, standing erect as if I was his superior, and his expression was not at all severe. He had a flabby, tired face, covered with wrinkles, with pouches under his eyes; his hair was dyed, and it was hard to guess his age from his appearance—fifty or sixty.

"I hope," he went on, "that you will appreciate Alexander Pavlovich's delicacy in applying to me, not officially, but privately. I have invited you unofficially not as a governor, but as a sincere admirer of your father's. And I ask you to change your conduct and to return to the duties proper to your rank, or, to avoid the evil effects of your example, to go to some other place where you are not known and where you may do what you like. Otherwise I shall have to resort to extreme measures."

For half a minute he stood in silence staring at me open-mouthed.

"Are you a vegetarian?" he asked.

"No, your Excellency, I eat meat."

He sat down and took up a document, and I bowed and left.

It was not worth while going to work before dinner. I went home and tried to sleep, but could not because of the unpleasant, sickly feeling from the slaughter-house and my conversation with the governor. And so I dragged through till the evening and then, feeling gloomy and out of sorts, I went to see Maria Victorovna. I told her about my visit to the governor and she looked at me in bewilderment, as if she did not believe me, and suddenly she began to laugh merrily, heartily, stridently, as only good-natured, light-hearted people can.

"If I were to tell this in Petersburg!" she cried, nearly dropping with laughter, bending over the table. "If I could tell them in Petersburg!"

IX

Now we saw each other often, sometimes twice a day. Almost every day, after dinner, she drove up to the cemetery and, as she waited for me, read the inscriptions on the crosses and monuments. Sometimes she came into the church and stood by my side and watched me working. The silence, the simple industry of the painters and gilders, Radish's good sense, and the fact that outwardly I was no different from the other artisans and worked as they did, in a waistcoat and old shoes, and that they addressed me familiarly—were new to her, and she was moved by it all. Once in her presence a painter who was working, at a door on the roof, called down to me:

"Misail, fetch me the white lead."

I fetched him the white lead and as I came down the scaffolding she was moved to tears and looked at me and smiled:

"What a dear you are!" she said.

I have always remembered how when I was a child a green parrot got out of its cage in one of the rich people's houses and wandered about the town for a whole month, flying from one garden to another, homeless and lonely. And Maria Victorovna reminded me of the bird.

"Except to the cemetery," she said with a laugh, "I have absolutely nowhere to go. The town bores me to tears. People read, sing, and twitter at the Azhoguins', but I cannot bear them lately. Your sister is shy, Miss Blagovo for some reason hates me. I don't like the theatre. What can I do with myself?"

When I was at her house I smelled of paint and turpentine, and my hands were stained. She liked that. She wanted me to come to her in my ordinary working-clothes; but I felt awkward in them in her drawing-room, and as if I were in uniform, and so I always wore my new serge suit. She did not like that.

"You must confess," she said once, "that you have not got used to your new rôle. A working-man's suit makes you feel awkward and embarrassed. Tell me, isn't it because you are not sure of yourself and are unsatisfied? Does this work you have chosen, this painting of yours, really satisfy you?" she asked merrily. "I know paint makes things look nicer and wear better, but the things themselves belong to the rich and after all they are a luxury. Besides you have said more than once that everybody should earn his living with his own hands and you earn money, not bread. Why don't you keep to the exact meaning of what you say? You must earn bread, real bread, you must plough, sow, reap, thrash, or do something which has to do directly with agriculture, such as keeping cows, digging, or building houses...."

She opened a handsome bookcase which stood by the writing-table and said:

"I'm telling you all this because I'm going to let you into my secret. Voilà. This is my agricultural library. Here are books on arable land, vegetable-gardens, orchard-keeping, cattle-keeping, bee-keeping: I read them eagerly and have studied the theory of everything thoroughly. It is my dream to go to Dubechnia as soon as March begins. It is wonderful there, amazing; isn't it? The first year I shall only be learning the work and getting used to it, and in the second year I shall begin to work thoroughly, without sparing myself. My father promised to give me Dubechnia as a present, and I am to do anything I like with it."

She blushed and with mingled laughter and tears she dreamed aloud of her life at Dubechnia and how absorbing it would be. And I envied her. March would soon be here. The days were drawing out, and in the bright sunny afternoons the snow dripped from the roofs, and the smell of spring was in the air. I too longed for the country.

And when she said she was going to live at Dubechnia, I saw at once that I should be left alone in the town, and I felt jealous of the bookcase with her books about farming. I knew and cared nothing about farming and I was on the point of telling her that agriculture was work for slaves, but I recollected that my father had once said something of the sort and I held my peace.

Lent began. The engineer, Victor Ivanich, came home from Petersburg. I had begun to forget his existence. He came unexpectedly, not even sending a telegram. When I went there as usual in the evening, he was walking up and down the drawing-room, after a bath, with his hair cut, looking ten years younger, and talking. His daughter was kneeling by his trunks and taking out boxes, bottles, books, and handing them to Pavel the footman. When I saw the engineer, I involuntarily stepped back and he held out both his hands and smiled and showed his strong, white, cab-driver's teeth.

"Here he is! Here he is! I'm very pleased to see you, Mr. House-painter! Maria told me all about you and sang your praises. I quite understand you and heartily approve." He took me by the arm and went on: "It is much cleverer and more honest to be a decent workman than to spoil State paper and to wear a cockade. I myself worked with my hands in Belgium. I was an engine-driver for five years...."

He was wearing a short jacket and comfortable slippers, and he shuffled along like a gouty man waving and rubbing his hands; humming and buzzing and shrugging with pleasure at being at home again with his favourite shower-bath.

"There's no denying," he said at supper, "there's no denying that you are kind, sympathetic people, but somehow as soon as you gentlefolk take on manual labour or try to spare the peasants, you reduce it all to sectarianism. You are a sectarian. You don't drink vodka. What is that but sectarianism?"

To please him I drank vodka. I drank wine, too. We ate cheese, sausages, pastries, pickles, and all kinds of dainties that the engineer had brought with him, and we sampled wines sent from abroad during his absence. They were excellent. For some reason the engineer had wines and cigars sent from abroad—duty free; somebody sent him caviare and baliki gratis; he did not pay rent for his house because his landlord supplied the railway with kerosene, and generally he and his daughter gave me the impression of having all the best things in the world at their service free of charge.

I went on visiting them, but with less pleasure than before. The engineer oppressed me and I felt cramped in his presence. I could not endure his clear, innocent eyes; his opinions bored me and were offensive to me, and I was distressed by the recollection that I had so recently been subordinate to this ruddy, well-fed man, and that he had been mercilessly rude to me. True he would put his arm round my waist and clap me kindly on the shoulder and approve of my way of living, but I felt that he despised my nullity just as much as before and only suffered me to please his daughter, but I could no longer laugh and talk easily, and I thought myself ill-mannered, and all the time was expecting him to call me Panteley as he did his footman Pavel. How my provincial, bourgeois pride rode up against him! I, a working man, a painter, going every day to the house of rich strangers, whom the whole town regarded as foreigners, and drinking their expensive wines and outlandish dishes! I could not reconcile this with my conscience. When I went to see them I sternly avoided those whom I met on the way, and looked askance at them like a real sectarian, and when I left the engineer's house I was ashamed of feeling so well-fed.

But chiefly I was afraid of falling in love. Whether walking in the street, or working, or talking to my mates, I thought all the time of going to Maria Victorovna's in the evening, and always had her voice, her laughter, her movements with me. And always as I got ready to go to her, I would stand for a long time in front of the cracked mirror tying my necktie; my serge suit seemed horrible to me, and I suffered, but at the same time, despised myself for feeling so small. When she called to me from another room to say that she was not dressed yet and to ask me to wait a bit, and I could hear her dressing, I was agitated and felt as though the floor was sinking under me. And when I saw a woman in the street, even at a distance, I fell to comparing her figure with hers, and it seemed to me that all our women and girls were vulgar, absurdly dressed, and without manners; and such comparisons roused in me a feeling of pride; Maria Victorovna was better than all of them. And at night I dreamed of her and myself.

Once at supper the engineer and I ate a whole lobster. When I reached home I remember that the engineer had twice called me "my dear fellow," and I thought that they treated me as they might have done a big, unhappy dog, separated from his master, and that they were amusing themselves with me, and that they would order me away like a dog when they were bored with me. I began to feel ashamed and hurt; went to the point of tears, as though I had been insulted, and, raising my eyes to the heavens, I vowed to put an end to it all.

Next day I did not go to the Dolyhikovs'. Late at night, when it was quite dark and pouring with rain, I walked up and down Great Gentry Street, looking at the windows. At the Azhoguins' everybody was asleep and the only light was in one of the top windows; old Mrs. Azhoguin was sitting in her room embroidering by candle-light and imagining herself to be fighting against prejudice. It was dark in our house and opposite, at the Dolyhikovs' the windows were lit up, but it was impossible to see anything through the flowers and curtains. I kept on walking up and down the street; I was soaked through with the cold March rain. I heard my father come home from the club; he knocked at the door; in a minute a light appeared at a window and I saw my sister walking quickly with her lamp and hurriedly arranging her thick hair. Then my father paced up and down the drawing-room, talking and rubbing his hands, and my sister sat still in a corner, lost in thought, not listening to him....

But soon they left the room and the light was put out.... I looked at the engineer's house and that too was now dark. In the darkness and the rain I felt desperately lonely. Cast out at the mercy of Fate, and I felt how, compared with my loneliness, and my suffering, actual and to come, all my work and all my desires and all that I had hitherto thought and read, were vain and futile. Alas!

The activities and thoughts of human beings are not nearly so important as their sorrows! And not knowing exactly what I was doing I pulled with all my might at the bell at the Dolyhikovs' gate, broke it, and ran away down the street like a little boy, full of fear, thinking they would rush out at once and recognise me. When I stopped to take breath at the end of the street, I could hear nothing but the falling rain and far away a night-watchman knocking on a sheet of iron.

For a whole week I did not go to the Dolyhikovs'. I sold my serge suit. I had no work and I was once more half-starved, earning ten or twenty copecks a day, when possible, by disagreeable work. Floundering knee-deep in the mire, putting out all my strength, I tried to drown my memories and to punish myself for all the cheeses and pickles to which I had been treated at the engineer's. Still, no sooner did I go to bed, wet and hungry, than my untamed imagination set to work to evolve wonderful, alluring pictures, and to my amazement I confessed that I was in love, passionately in love, and I fell sound asleep feeling that the hard life had only made my body stronger and younger.

One evening it began, most unseasonably, to snow, and the wind blew from the north, exactly as if winter had begun again. When I got home from work I found Maria Victorovna in my room. She was in her furs with her hands in her muff.

"Why don't you come to see me?" she asked, looking at me with her bright sagacious eyes, and I was overcome with joy and stood stiffly in front of her, just as I had done with my father when he was going to thrash me; she looked straight into my face and I could see by her eyes that she understood why I was overcome.

"Why don't you come to see me?" she repeated. "You don't want to come? I had to come to you."

She got up and came close to me.

"Don't leave me," she said, and her eyes filled with tears. "I am lonely, utterly lonely."

She began to cry and said, covering her face with her muff:

"Alone! Life is hard, very hard, and in the whole world I have no one but you. Don't leave me!"

Looking for her handkerchief to dry her tears, she gave a smile; we were silent for some time, then I embraced and kissed her, and the pin in her hat scratched my face and drew blood.

And we began to talk as though we had been dear to each other for a long, long time.

X

In a couple of days she sent me to Dubechnia and I was beyond words delighted with it. As I walked to the station, and as I sat in the train, I laughed for no reason and people thought me drunk. There were snow and frost in the mornings still, but the roads were getting dark, and there were rooks cawing above them.

At first I thought of arranging the side wing opposite Mrs. Cheprakov's for myself and Masha, but it appeared that doves and pigeons had taken up their abode there and it would be impossible to cleanse it without destroying a great number of nests. We would have to live willy-nilly in the uncomfortable rooms with Venetian blinds in the big house. The peasants called it a palace; there were more than twenty rooms in it, and the only furniture was a piano and a child's chair, lying in the attic, and even if Masha brought all her furniture from town we should not succeed in removing the impression of frigid emptiness and coldness. I chose three small rooms with windows looking on to the garden, and from early morning till late at night I was at work in them, glazing the windows, hanging paper, blocking up the chinks and holes in the floor. It was an easy, pleasant job. Every now and then I would run to the river to see if the ice was breaking and all the while I dreamed of the starlings returning. And at night when I thought of Masha I would be filled with an inexpressibly sweet feeling of an all-embracing joy to listen to the rats and the wind rattling and knocking above the ceiling; it was like an old hobgoblin coughing in the attic.

The snow was deep; there was a heavy fall at the end of March, but it thawed rapidly, as if by magic, and the spring floods rushed down so that by the beginning of April the starlings were already chattering and yellow butterflies fluttered in the garden. The weather was wonderful. Every day toward evening I walked toward the town to meet Masha, and how delightful it was to walk along the soft, drying road with bare feet! Half-way I would sit down and look at the town, not daring to go nearer. The sight of it upset me, I was always wondering how my acquaintances would behave toward me when they heard of my love. What would my father say? I was particularly worried by the idea that my life was becoming more complicated, and that I had entirely lost control of it, and that she was carrying me off like a balloon, God knows whither. I had already given up thinking how to make a living, and I thought—indeed, I cannot remember what I thought.

Masha used to come in a carriage. I would take a seat beside her and together, happy and free, we used to drive to Dubechnia. Or, having waited till sunset, I would return home, weary and disconsolate, wondering why Masha had not come, and then by the gate or in the garden I would find my darling. She would come by the railway and walk over from the station. What a triumph she had then! In her plain, woollen dress, with a simple umbrella, but keeping a trim, fashionable figure and expensive, Parisian boots—she was a gifted actress playing the country girl. We used to go over the house, and plan out the rooms, and the paths, and the vegetable-garden, and the beehives. We already had chickens and ducks and geese which we loved because they were ours. We had oats, clover, buckwheat, and vegetable seeds all ready for sowing, and we used to examine them all and wonder what the crops would be like, and everything Masha said to me seemed extraordinarily clever and fine. This was the happiest time of my life.

Soon after Easter we were married in the parish church in the village of Kurilovka three miles from Dubechnia. Masha wanted everything to be simple; by her wish our bridesmen were peasant boys, only one deacon sang, and we returned from the church in a little, shaky cart which she drove herself. My sister was the only guest from the town. Masha had sent her a note a couple of days before the wedding. My sister wore a white dress and white gloves.... During the ceremony she cried softly for joy and emotion, and her face had a maternal expression of infinite goodness. She was intoxicated with our happiness and smiled as though she were breathing a sweet perfume, and when I looked at her I understood that there was nothing in the world higher in her eyes than love, earthly love, and that she was always dreaming of love, secretly, timidly, yet passionately. She embraced Masha and kissed her, and, not knowing how to express her ecstasy, she said to her of me:

"He is a good man! A very good man."

Before she left us, she put on her ordinary clothes, and took me into the garden to have a quiet talk.

"Father is very hurt that you have not written to him," she said. "You should have asked for his blessing. But, at heart, he is very pleased. He says that this marriage will raise you in the eyes of society, and that under Maria Victorovna's influence you will begin to adopt a more serious attitude toward life. In the evening now we talk about nothing but you; and yesterday he even said, 'our Misail.' I was delighted. He has evidently thought of a plan and I believe he wants to set you an example of magnanimity, and that he will be the first to talk of reconciliation. It is quite possible that one of these days he will come and see you here."

She made the sign of the cross over me and said:

"Well, God bless you. Be happy. Aniuta Blagovo is a very clever girl. She says of your marriage that God has sent you a new ordeal. Well? Married life is not made up only of joy but of suffering as well. It is impossible to avoid it."

Masha and I walked about three miles with her, and then walked home quietly and silently, as though it were a rest for both of us. Masha had her hand on my arm. We were at peace and there was no need to talk of love; after the wedding we grew closer to each other and dearer, and it seemed as though nothing could part us.

"Your sister is a dear, lovable creature," said Masha, "but looks as though she had lived in torture. Your father must be a terrible man."

I began to tell her how my sister and I had been brought up and how absurd and full of torture our childhood had been. When she heard that my father had thrashed me quite recently she shuddered and clung to me:

"Don't tell me any more," she said. "It is too horrible."

And now she did not leave me. We lived in the big house, in three rooms, and in the evenings we bolted the door that led to the empty part of the house, as though some one lived there whom we did not know and feared. I used to get up early, at dawn, and begin working. I repaired the carts; made paths in the garden, dug the beds, painted the roofs. When the time came to sow oats, I tried to plough and harrow, and sow and did it all conscientiously, and did not leave it all to the labourer. I used to get tired, and my face and feet used to burn with the rain and the sharp cold wind. But work in the fields did not attract me. I knew nothing about agriculture and did not like it; perhaps because my ancestors were not tillers of the soil and pure town blood ran in my veins. I loved nature dearly; I loved the fields and the meadows and the garden, but the peasant who turns the earth with his plough, shouting at his miserable horse, ragged and wet, with bowed shoulders, was to me an expression of wild, rude, ugly force, and as I watched his clumsy movements I could not help thinking of the long-passed legendary life, when men did not yet know the use of fire. The fierce bull which led the herd, and the horses that stampeded through the village, filled me with terror, and all the large creatures, strong and hostile, a ram with horns, a gander, or a watch-dog seemed to me to be symbolical of some rough, wild force. These prejudices used to be particularly strong in me in bad weather, when heavy clouds hung over the black plough-lands. But worst of all was that when I was ploughing or sowing, and a few peasants stood and watched how I did it, I no longer felt the inevitability and necessity of the work and it seemed to me that I was trifling my time away.

I used to go through the gardens and the meadow to the mill. It was leased by Stiepan, a Kurilovka peasant; handsome, swarthy, with a black beard—an athletic appearance. He did not care for mill work and thought it tiresome and unprofitable, and he only lived at the mill to escape from home. He was a saddler and always smelled of tan and leather. He did not like talking, was slow and immovable, and used to hum "U-lu-lu-lu," sitting on the bank or in the doorway of the mill. Sometimes his wife and mother-in-law used to come from Kurilovka to see him; they were both fair, languid, soft, and they used to bow to him humbly and call him Stiepan Petrovich. And he would not answer their greeting with a word or a sign, but would turn where he sat on the bank and hum quietly: "U-lu-lu-lu." There would be a silence for an hour or two. His mother-in-law and his wife would whisper to each other, get up and look expectantly at him for some time, waiting for him to look at them, and then they would bow humbly and say in sweet, soft voices:

"Good-bye, Stiepan Petrovich."

And they would go away. After that, Stiepan would put away the bundle of cracknels or the shirt they had left for him and sigh and give a wink in their direction and say:

"The female sex!"

The mill was worked with both wheels day and night. I used to help Stiepan, I liked it, and when he went away I was glad to take his place.

XI

After a spell of warm bright weather we had a season of bad roads. It rained and was cold all through May. The grinding of the millstones and the drip of the rain induced idleness and sleep. The floor shook, the whole place smelled of flour, and this too made one drowsy. My wife in a short fur coat and high rubber boots used to appear twice a day and she always said the same thing:

"Call this summer! It is worse than October!"

We used to have tea together and cook porridge, or sit together for hours in silence thinking the rain would never stop. Once when Stiepan went away to a fair, Masha stayed the night in the mill. When we got up we could not tell what time it was for the sky was overcast; the sleepy cocks at Dubechnia were crowing, and the corncrakes were trilling in the meadow; it was very, very early.... My wife and I walked down to the pool and drew up the bow-net that Stiepan had put out in our presence the day before. There was one large perch in it and a crayfish angrily stretched out his claws.

"Let them go," said Masha. "Let them be happy too."

Because we got up very early and had nothing to do, the day seemed very long, the longest in my life. Stiepan returned before dusk and I went back to the farmhouse.

"Your father came here to-day," said Masha.

"Where is he?"

"He has gone. I did not receive him."

Seeing my silence and feeling that I was sorry for my father, she said:

"We must be logical. I did not receive him and sent a message to ask him not to trouble us again and not to come and see us."

In a moment I was outside the gates, striding toward the town to make it up with my father. It was muddy, slippery, cold. For the first time since our marriage I suddenly felt sad, and through my brain, tired with the long day, there flashed the thought that perhaps I was not living as I ought; I got more and more tired and was gradually overcome with weakness, inertia; I had no desire to move or to think, and after walking for some time, I waved my hand and went home.

In the middle of the yard stood the engineer in a leather coat with a hood. He was shouting:

"Where's the furniture? There was some good Empire furniture, pictures, vases. There's nothing left! Damn it, I bought the place with the furniture!"

Near him stood Moissey, Mrs. Cheprakov's bailiff, fumbling with his cap; a lank fellow of about twenty-five, with a spotty face and little, impudent eyes; one side of his face was larger than the other as though he had been lain on.

"Yes, Right Honourable Sir, you bought it without the furniture," he said sheepishly. "I remember that clearly."

"Silence!" shouted the engineer, going red in the face, and beginning to shake, and his shout echoed through the garden.

XII

When I was busy in the garden or the yard, Moissey would stand with his hands behind his back and stare at me impertinently with his little eyes. And this used to irritate me to such an extent that I would put aside my work and go away.

We learned from Stiepan that Moissey had been Mrs. Cheprakov's lover. I noticed that when people went to her for money they used to apply to Moissey first, and once I saw a peasant, a charcoal-burner, black all over, grovel at his feet. Sometimes after a whispered conversation Moissey would hand over the money himself without saying anything to his mistress, from which I concluded that the transaction was settled on his own account.

He used to shoot in our garden, under our very windows, steal food from our larder, borrow our horses without leave, and we were furious, feeling that Dubechnia was no longer ours, and Masha used to go pale and say:

"Have we to live another year and a half with these creatures?"

Ivan Cheprakov, the son, was a guard on the railway. During the winter he got very thin and weak, so that he got drunk on one glass of vodka, and felt cold out of the sun. He hated wearing his guard's uniform and was ashamed of it, but found his job profitable because he could steal candles and sell them. My new position gave him a mixed feeling of astonishment, envy, and vague hope that something of the sort might happen to him. He used to follow Masha with admiring eyes, and to ask me what I had for dinner nowadays, and his ugly, emaciated face used to wear a sweet, sad expression, and he used to twitch his fingers as though he could feel my happiness with them.

"I say, Little Profit," he would say excitedly, lighting and relighting his cigarette; he always made a mess wherever he stood because he used to waste a whole box of matches on one cigarette. "I say, my life is about as beastly as it could be. Every little squirt of a soldier can shout: 'Here guard! Here!' I have such a lot in the trains and you know, mine's a rotten life! My mother has ruined me! I heard a doctor say in the train, if the parents are loose, their children become drunkards or criminals. That's it."

Once he came staggering into the yard. His eyes wandered aimlessly and he breathed heavily; he laughed and cried, and said something in a kind of frenzy, and through his thickly uttered words I could only hear: "My mother? Where is my mother?" and he wailed like a child crying, because it has lost its mother in a crowd. I led him away into the garden and laid him down under a tree, and all that day and through the night Masha and I took it in turns to stay with him. He was sick and Masha looked with disgust at his pale, wet face and said:

"Are we to have these creatures on the place for another year and a half? It is awful! Awful!"

And what a lot of trouble the peasants gave us! How many disappointments we had at the outset, in the spring, when we so longed to be happy! My wife built a school. I designed the school for sixty boys, and the Zemstvo Council approved the design, but recommended our building the school at Kurilovka, the big village, only three miles away; besides the Kurilovka school, where the children of four villages, including that of Dubechnia, were taught, was old and inadequate and the floor was so rotten that the children were afraid to walk on it. At the end of March Masha, by her own desire, was appointed trustee of the Kurilovka school, and at the beginning of April we called three parish meetings and persuaded the peasants that the school was old and inadequate, and that it was necessary to build a new one. A member of the Zemstvo Council and the elementary school inspector came down too and addressed them. After each meeting we were mobbed and asked for a pail of vodka; we felt stifled in the crowd and soon got tired and returned home dissatisfied and rather abashed. At last the peasants allotted a site for the school and undertook to cart the materials from the town. And as soon as the spring corn was sown, on the very first Sunday, carts set out from Kurilovka and Dubechnia to fetch the bricks for the foundations. They went at dawn and returned late in the evening. The peasants were drunk and said they were tired out.

The rain and the cold continued, as though deliberately, all through May. The roads were spoiled and deep in mud. When the carts came from town they usually drove to our horror, into our yard! A horse would appear in the gate, straddling its fore legs, with its big belly heaving; before it came into the yard it would strain and heave and after it would come a ten-yard beam in a four-wheeled wagon, wet and slimy; alongside it, wrapped up to keep the rain out, never looking where he was going and splashing through the puddles, a peasant would walk with the skirt of his coat tucked up in his belt. Another cart would appear with planks; then a third with a beam; then a fourth ... and the yard in front of the house would gradually be blocked up with horses, beams, planks. Peasants, men and women with their heads wrapped up and their skirts tucked up, would stare morosely at our windows, kick up a row and insist on the lady of the house coming out to them; and they would curse and swear. And in a corner Moissey would stand, and it seemed to us that he delighted in our discomfiture.

"We won't cart any more!" the peasants shouted. "We are tired to death! Let her go and cart it herself!"

Pale and scared, thinking they would any minute break into the house, Masha would send them money for a pail of vodka; after which the noise would die down and the long beams would go jolting out of the yard.

When I went to look at the building my wife would get agitated and say:

"The peasants are furious. They might do something to you. No. Wait. I'll go with you."

We used to drive over to Kurilovka together and then the carpenters would ask for tips. The framework was ready for the foundations to be laid, but the masons never came and when at last the masons did come it was apparent that there was no sand; somehow it had been forgotten that sand was wanted. Taking advantage of our helplessness, the peasants asked thirty copecks a load, although it was less than a quarter of a mile from the building to the river where the sand was to be fetched, and more than five hundred loads were needed. There were endless misunderstandings, wrangles, and continual begging. My wife was indignant and the building contractor, Petrov, an old man of seventy, took her by the hand and said:

"You look here! Look here! Just get me sand and I'll find ten men and have the work done in two days. Look here!"

Sand was brought, but two, four days, a week passed and still there yawned a ditch where the foundations were to be.

"I shall go mad," cried my wife furiously. "What wretches they are! What wretches!"

During these disturbances Victor Ivanich used to come and see us. He used to bring hampers of wine and dainties, and eat for a long time, and then go to sleep on the terrace and snore so that the labourers shook their heads and said:

"He's all right!"

Masha took no pleasure in his visits. She did not believe in him, and yet she used to ask his advice; when, after a sound sleep after dinner, he got up out of humour, and spoke disparagingly of our domestic arrangements, and said he was sorry he had ever bought Dubechnia which had cost him so much, and poor Masha looked miserably anxious and complained to him, he would yawn and say the peasants ought to be flogged.

He called our marriage and the life we were living a comedy, and used to say it was a caprice, a whimsy.

"She did the same sort of thing once before," he told me. "She fancied herself as an opera singer, and ran away from me. It took me two months to find her, and my dear fellow, I wasted a thousand roubles on telegrams alone."

He had dropped calling me a sectarian or the House-painter; and no longer approved of my life as a working man, but he used to say:

"You are a queer fish! An abnormality. I don't venture to prophesy, but you will end badly!"

Masha slept poorly at nights and would sit by the window of our bedroom thinking. She no longer laughed and made faces at supper. I suffered, and when it rained, every drop cut into my heart like a bullet, and I could have gone on my knees to Masha and apologised for the weather. When the peasants made a row in the yard, I felt that it was my fault. I would sit for hours in one place, thinking only how splendid and how wonderful Masha was. I loved her passionately, and I was enraptured by everything she did and said. Her taste was for quiet indoor occupation; she loved to read for hours and to study; she who knew about farm-work only from books, surprised us all by her knowledge and the advice she gave was always useful, and when applied was never in vain. And in addition she had the fineness, the taste, and the good sense, the very sound sense which only very well-bred people possess!

To such a woman, with her healthy, orderly mind, the chaotic environment with its petty cares and dirty tittle-tattle, in which we lived, was very painful. I could see that, and I, too, could not sleep at night. My brain whirled and I could hardly choke back my tears. I tossed about, not knowing what to do.

I used to rush to town and bring Masha books, newspapers, sweets, flowers, and I used to go fishing with Stiepan, dragging for hours, neck-deep in cold water, in the rain, to catch an eel by way of varying our fare. I used humbly to ask the peasants not to shout, and I gave them vodka, bribed them, promised them anything they asked. And what a lot of other foolish things I did!

At last the rain stopped. The earth dried up. I used to get up in the morning and go into the garden—dew shining on the flowers, birds and insects shrilling, not a cloud in the sky, and the garden, the meadow, the river were so beautiful, perfect but for the memory of the peasants and the carts and the engineer. Masha and I used to drive out in a car to see how the oats were coming on. She drove and I sat behind; her shoulders were always a little hunched, and the wind would play with her hair.

"Keep to the right!" she shouted to the passers-by.

"You are like a coachman!" I once said to her.

"Perhaps. My grandfather, my father's father, was a coachman. Didn't you know?" she asked, turning round, and immediately she began to mimic the way the coachmen shout and sing.

"Thank God!" I thought, as I listened to her. "Thank God!"

And again I remember the peasants, the carts, the engineer....

XIII

Doctor Blagovo came over on a bicycle. My sister began to come often. Once more we talked of manual labour and progress, and the mysterious Cross awaiting humanity in the remote future. The doctor did not like our life, because it interfered with our discussions and he said it was unworthy of a free man to plough, and reap, and breed cattle, and that in time all such elementary forms of the struggle for existence would be left to animals and machines, while men would devote themselves exclusively to scientific investigation. And my sister always asked me to let her go home earlier, and if she stayed late, or for the night, she was greatly distressed.

"Good gracious, what a baby you are," Masha used to say reproachfully. "It is quite ridiculous."

"Yes, it is absurd," my sister would agree. "I admit it is absurd, but what can I do if I have not the power to control myself. It always seems to me that I am doing wrong."

During the haymaking my body, not being used to it, ached all over; sitting on the terrace in the evening, I would suddenly fall asleep and they would all laugh at me. They would wake me up and make me sit down to supper. I would be overcome with drowsiness and in a stupor saw lights, faces, plates, and heard voices without understanding what they were saying. And I used to get up early in the morning and take my scythe, or go to the school and work there all day.

When I was at home on holidays I noticed that my wife and sister were hiding something from me and even seemed to be avoiding me. My wife was tender with me as always, but she had some new thought of her own which she did not communicate to me. Certainly her exasperation with the peasants had increased and life was growing harder and harder for her, but she no longer complained to me. She talked more readily to the doctor than to me, and I could not understand why.

It was the custom in our province for the labourers to come to the farm in the evenings to be treated to vodka, even the girls having a glass. We did not keep the custom; the haymakers and the women used to come into the yard and stay until late in the evening, waiting for vodka, and then they went away cursing. And then Masha used to frown and relapse into silence or whisper irritably to the doctor:

"Savages! Barbarians!"

Newcomers to the villages were received ungraciously, almost with hostility; like new arrivals at a school. At first we were looked upon as foolish, soft-headed people who had bought the estate because we did not know what to do with our money. We were laughed at. The peasants grazed their cattle in our pasture and even in our garden, drove our cows and horses into the village and then came and asked for compensation. The whole village used to come into our yard and declare loudly that in mowing we had cut the border of common land which did not belong to us; and as we did not know our boundaries exactly we used to take their word for it and pay a fine. But afterward it appeared that we had been in the right. They used to bark the young lime-trees in our woods. A Dubechnia peasant, a money-lender, who sold vodka without a licence, bribed our labourers to help him cheat us in the most treacherous way; he substituted old wheels for the new on our wagons, stole our ploughing yokes and sold them back to us, and so on. But worst of all was the building at Kurilovka. There the women at night stole planks, bricks, tiles, iron; the bailiff and his assistants made a search; the women were each fined two roubles by the village council, and then the whole lot of them got drunk on the money.

When Masha found out, she would say to the doctor and my sister:

"What beasts! It is horrible! Horrible!"

And more than once I heard her say she was sorry she had decided to build the school.

"You must understand," the doctor tried to point out, "that if you build a school or undertake any good work, it is not for the peasants, but for the sake of culture and the future. The worse the peasants are the more reason there is for building a school. Do understand!"

There was a loss of confidence in his voice, and it seemed to me that he hated the peasants as much as Masha.

Masha used often to go to the mill with my sister and they would say jokingly that they were going to have a look at Stiepan because he was so handsome. Stiepan it appeared was reserved and silent only with men, and in the company of women was free and talkative. Once when I went down to the river to bathe I involuntarily overheard a conversation. Masha and Cleopatra, both in white, were sitting on the bank under the broad shade of a willow and Stiepan was standing near with his hands behind his back, saying:

"But are peasants human beings? Not they; they are, excuse me, brutes, beasts, and thieves. What does a peasant's life consist of? Eating and drinking, crying for cheaper food, bawling in taverns, without decent conversation, or behaviour or manners. Just an ignorant beast! He lives in filth, his wife and children live in filth; he sleeps in his clothes; takes the potatoes out of the soup with his fingers, drinks down a black beetle with his kvass—because he won't trouble to fish it out!"

"It is because of their poverty!" protested my sister.

"What poverty? Of course there is want, but there are different kinds of necessity. If a man is in prison, or is blind, say, or has lost his legs, then he is in a bad way and God help him; but if he is at liberty and in command of his senses, if he has eyes and hands and strength, then, good God, what more does he want? It is lamentable, my lady, ignorance, but not poverty. If you kind people, with your education, out of charity try to help him, then he will spend your money in drink, like the swine he is, or worse still, he will open a tavern and begin to rob the people on the strength of your money. You say—poverty. But does a rich peasant live any better? He lives like a pig, too, excuse me, a clodhopper, a blusterer, a big-bellied blockhead, with a swollen red mug—makes me want to hit him in the eye, the blackguard. Look at Larion of Dubechnia—he is rich, but all the same he barks the trees in your woods just like the poor; and he is a foul-mouthed brute, and his children are foul-mouthed, and when he is drunk he falls flat in the mud and goes to sleep. They are all worthless, my lady. It is just hell to live with them in the village. The village sticks in my gizzard, and I thank God, the King of heaven, that I am well fed and clothed, and that I am a free man; I can live where I like, I don't want to live in the village and nobody can force me to do it. They say: 'You have a wife.' They say: 'You are obliged to live at home with your wife.' Why? I have not sold myself to her."

"Tell me, Stiepan. Did you marry for love?" asked Masha.

"What love is there in a village?" Stiepan answered with a smile. "If you want to know, my lady, it is my second marriage. I do not come from Kurilovka, but from Zalegosch, and I went to Kurilovka when I married. My father did not want to divide the land up between us—there are five of us. So I bowed to it and cut adrift and went to another village to my wife's family. My first wife died when she was young."

"What did she die of?"

"Foolishness. She used to sit and cry. She was always crying for no reason at all and so she wasted away. She used to drink herbs to make herself prettier and it must have ruined her inside. And my second wife at Kurilovka—what about her? A village woman, a peasant; that's all. When the match was being made I was nicely had; I thought she was young, nice to look at and clean. Her mother was clean enough, drank coffee and, chiefly because they were a clean lot, I got married. Next day we sat down to dinner and I told my mother-in-law to fetch me a spoon. She brought me a spoon and I saw her wipe it with her finger. So that, thought I, is their cleanliness! I lived with them for a year and went away. Perhaps I ought to have married a town girl"—he went on after a silence. "They say a wife is a helpmate to her husband. What do I want with a helpmate? I can look after myself. But you talk to me sensibly and soberly, without giggling all the while. He—he—he! What is life without a good talk?"

Stiepan suddenly stopped and relapsed into his dreary, monotonous "U-lu-lu-lu." That meant that he had noticed me.

Masha used often to visit the mill, she evidently took pleasure in her talks with Stiepan; he abused the peasants so sincerely and convincingly—and this attracted her to him. When she returned from the mill the idiot who looked after the garden used to shout after her:

"Paloshka! Hullo, Paloshka!" And he would bark at her like a dog: "Bow, wow!"

And she would stop and stare at him as if she found in the idiot's barking an answer to her thought, and perhaps he attracted her as much as Stiepan's abuse. And at home she would find some unpleasant news awaiting her, as that the village geese had ruined the cabbages in the kitchen-garden, or that Larion had stolen the reins, and she would shrug her shoulders with a smile and say:

"What can you expect of such people?"

She was exasperated and a fury was gathering in her soul, and I, on the other hand, was getting used to the peasants and more and more attracted to them. For the most part, they were nervous, irritable, absurd people; they were people with suppressed imaginations, ignorant, with a bare, dull outlook, always dazed by the same thought of the grey earth, grey days, black bread; they were people driven to cunning, but, like birds, they only hid their heads behind the trees—they could not reason. They did not come to us for the twenty roubles earned by haymaking, but for the half-pail of vodka, though they could buy four pails of vodka for the twenty roubles. Indeed they were dirty, drunken, and dishonest, but for all that one felt that the peasant life as a whole was sound at the core. However clumsy and brutal the peasant might look as he followed his antiquated plough, and however he might fuddle himself with vodka, still, looking at him more closely, one felt that there was something vital and important in him, something that was lacking in Masha and the doctor, for instance, namely, that he believes that the chief thing on earth is truth, that his and everybody's salvation lies in truth, and therefore above all else on earth he loves justice. I used to say to my wife that she was seeing the stain on the window, but not the glass itself; and she would be silent or, like Stiepan, she would hum, "U-lu-lu-lu...." When she, good, clever actress that she was, went pale with fury and then harangued the doctor in a trembling voice about drunkenness and dishonesty; her blindness confounded and appalled me. How could she forget that her father, the engineer, drank, drank heavily, and that the money with which he bought Dubechnia was acquired by means of a whole series of impudent, dishonest swindles? How could she forget?

XIV

And my sister, too, was living with her own private thoughts which she hid from me. She used often to sit whispering with Masha. When I went up to her, she would shrink away, and her eyes would look guilty and full of entreaty. Evidently there was something going on in her soul of which she was afraid or ashamed. To avoid meeting me in the garden or being left alone with me she clung to Masha and I hardly ever had a chance to talk to her except at dinner.

One evening, on my way home from the school, I came quietly through the garden. It had already begun to grow dark. Without noticing me or hearing footsteps, my sister walked round an old wide-spreading apple-tree, perfectly noiselessly like a ghost. She was in black, and walked very quickly, up and down, up and down, with her eyes on the ground. An apple fell from the tree, she started at the noise, stopped and pressed her hands to her temples. At that moment I went up to her.

In an impulse of tenderness, which suddenly came rushing to my heart, with tears in my eyes, somehow remembering our mother and our childhood, I took hold of her shoulders and kissed her.

"What is the matter?" I asked. "You are suffering. I have seen it for a long time now. Tell me, what is the matter?"

"I am afraid...." she murmured, with a shiver.

"What's the matter with you?" I inquired. "For God's sake, be frank!"

"I will, I will be frank. I will tell you the whole truth. It is so hard, so painful to conceal anything from you!... Misail, I am in love." She went on in a whisper. "Love, love.... I am happy, but I am afraid."

I heard footsteps and Doctor Blagovo appeared among the trees. He was wearing a silk shirt and high boots. Clearly they had arranged a rendezvous by the apple-tree. When she saw him she flung herself impulsively into his arms with a cry of anguish, as though he was being taken away from her:

"Vladimir! Vladimir!"

She clung to him, and gazed eagerly at him and only then I noticed how thin and pale she had become. It was especially noticeable through her lace collar, which I had known for years, for it now hung loosely about her slim neck. The doctor was taken aback, but controlled himself at once, and said, as he stroked her hair:

"That's enough. Enough!... Why are you so nervous? You see, I have come."

We were silent for a time, bashfully glancing at each other. Then we all moved away and I heard the doctor saying to me:

"Civilised life has not yet begun with us. The old console themselves with saying that, if there is nothing now, there was something in the forties and the sixties; that is all right for the old ones, but we are young and our brains are not yet touched with senile decay. We cannot console ourselves with such illusions. The beginning of Russia was in 862, and civilised Russia, as I understand it, has not yet begun."

But I could not bother about what he was saying. It was very strange, but I could not believe that my sister was in love, that she had just been walking with her hand on the arm of a stranger and gazing at him tenderly. My sister, poor, frightened, timid, downtrodden creature as she was, loved a man who was already married and had children! I was full of pity without knowing why; the doctor's presence was distasteful to me and I could not make out what was to come of such a love.

XV

Masha and I drove over to Kurilovka for the opening of the school.

"Autumn, autumn, autumn...." said Masha, looking about her.

128

Summer had passed. There were no birds and only the willows were green.

Yes. Summer had passed. The days were bright and warm, but it was fresh in the mornings; the shepherds went out in their sheep-skins, and the dew never dried all day on the asters in the garden. There were continual mournful sounds and it was impossible to tell whether it was a shutter creaking on its rusty hinges or the cranes flying—and one felt so well and so full of the desire for life!

"Summer has passed...." said Masha. "Now we can both make up our accounts. We have worked hard and thought a great deal and we are the better for it—all honour and praise to us; we have improved ourselves; but have our successes had any perceptible influence on the life around us, have they been of any use to a single person? No! Ignorance, dirt, drunkenness, a terribly high rate of infant mortality—everything is just as it was, and no one is any the better for your having ploughed and sown and my having spent money and read books. Evidently we have only worked and broadened our minds for ourselves."

I was abashed by such arguments and did not know what to think.

"From beginning to end we have been sincere," I said, "and if a man is sincere, he is right."

"Who denies that? We have been right but we have been wrong in our way of setting about it. First of all, are not our very ways of living wrong? You want to be useful to people, but by the mere fact of buying an estate you make it impossible to be so. Further, if you work, dress, and eat like a peasant you lend your authority and approval to the clumsy clothes, and their dreadful houses and their dirty beards.... On the other hand, suppose you work for a long, long time, all you life, and in the end obtain some practical results—what will your results amount to, what can they do against such elemental forces as wholesale ignorance, hunger, cold, and degeneracy? A drop in the ocean! Other methods of fighting are necessary, strong, bold, quick! If you want to be useful then you must leave the narrow circle of common activity and try to act directly on the masses! First of all, you need vigorous, noisy, propaganda. Why are art and music, for instance, so much alive and so popular and so powerful? Because the musician or the singer influences thousands directly. Art, wonderful art!" She looked wistfully at the sky and went on: "Art gives wings and carries you far, far away. If you are bored with dirt and pettifogging interests, if you are exasperated and outraged and indignant, rest and satisfaction are only to be found in beauty."

As we approached Kurilovka the weather was fine, clear, and joyous. In the yards the peasants were thrashing and there was a smell of corn and straw. Behind the wattled hedges the fruit-trees were reddening and all around the trees were red or golden. In the church-tower the bells were ringing, the children were carrying ikons to the school and singing the Litany of the Virgin. And how clear the air was, and how high the doves soared!

The Te Deum was sung in the schoolroom. Then the Kurilovka peasants presented Masha with an ikon, and the Dubechnia peasants gave her a large cracknel and a gilt salt-cellar. And Masha began to weep.

"And if we have said anything out of the way or have been discontented, please forgive us," said an old peasant, bowing to us both.

As we drove home Masha looked back at the school. The green roof which I had painted glistened in the sun, and we could see it for a long time. And I felt that Masha's glances were glances of farewell.

XVI

In the evening she got ready to go to town.

She had often been to town lately to stay the night. In her absence I could not work, and felt listless and disheartened; our big yard seemed dreary, disgusting, and deserted; there were ominous noises in the garden, and without her the house, the trees, the horses were no longer "ours."

I never went out but sat all the time at her writing-table among her books on farming and agriculture, those deposed favourites, wanted no more, which looked out at me so shamefacedly from the bookcase. For hours together, while it struck seven, eight, nine, and the autumn night crept up as black as soot to the windows, I sat brooding over an old glove of hers, or the pen she always used, and her little scissors. I did nothing and saw clearly that everything I had done before, ploughing, sowing, and felling trees, had only been because she wanted it. And if she told me to clean out a well, when I had to stand waist-deep in water, I would go and do it, without trying to find out whether the well wanted cleaning or not. And now, when she was away, Dubechnia with its squalor, its litter, its slamming shutters, with thieves prowling about it day and night, seemed to me like a chaos in which work was entirely useless. And why should I work, then? Why trouble and worry about the future, when I felt that the ground was slipping away from under me, that my position at Dubechnia was hollow, that, in a word, the same fate awaited me as had befallen the books on agriculture? Oh! what anguish it was at night, in the lonely hours, when I lay listening uneasily, as though I expected some one any minute to call out that it was time for me to go away. I was not sorry to leave Dubechnia, my sorrow was for my love, for which it seemed that autumn had already begun. What a tremendous happiness it is to love and to be loved, and what a horror it is to feel that you are beginning to topple down from that lofty tower!

Masha returned from town toward evening on the following day. She was dissatisfied with something, but concealed it and said only: "Why have the winter windows been put in? It will be stifling." I opened two of the windows. We did not feel like eating, but we sat down and had supper.

"Go and wash your hands," she said. "You smell of putty."

She had brought some new illustrated magazines from town and we both read them after supper. They had supplements with fashion-plates and patterns. Masha just glanced at them and put them aside to look at them carefully later on; but one dress, with a wide, bell-shaped skirt and big sleeves interested her, and for a moment she looked at it seriously and attentively.

"That's not bad," she said.

"Yes, it would suit you very well," said I. "Very well."

And I admired the dress, only because she liked it, and went on tenderly:

"A wonderful, lovely dress! Lovely, wonderful, Masha. My dear Masha!"

And tears began to drop on the fashion-plate.

"Wonderful Masha...." I murmured. "Dear, darling Masha...."

She went and lay down and I sat still for an hour and looked at the illustrations.

"You should not have opened the windows," she called from the bedroom. "I'm afraid it will be cold. Look how the wind is blowing in!"

I read the miscellany, about the preparation of cheap fish, and the size of the largest diamond in the world. Then I chanced on the picture of the dress she had liked and I imagined her at a ball, with a fan, and bare shoulders, a brilliant, dazzling figure, well up in music and painting and literature, and how insignificant and brief my share in her life seemed to be!

Our coming together, our marriage, was only an episode, one of many in the life of this lively, highly gifted creature. All the best things in the world, as I have said, were at her service, and she had them for nothing; even ideas and fashionable intellectual movements served her pleasure, a diversion in her existence, and I was only the coachman who drove her from one infatuation to another. Now I was no longer necessary to her; she would fly away and I should be left alone.

As if in answer to my thoughts a desperate scream suddenly came from the yard:

"Mur-der!"

It was a shrill female voice, and exactly as though it were trying to imitate it, the wind also howled dismally in the chimney. Half a minute passed and again it came through the sound of the wind, but as though from the other end of the yard:

"Mur-der!"

"Misail, did you hear that?" said my wife in a hushed voice. "Did you hear?"

She came out of the bedroom in her nightgown, with her hair down, and stood listening and staring out of the dark window.

"Somebody is being murdered!" she muttered. "It only wanted that!"

I took my gun and went out; it was very dark outside; a violent wind was blowing so that it was hard to stand up. I walked to the gate and listened; the trees were moaning; the wind went whistling through them, and in the garden the idiot's dog was howling. Beyond the gate it was pitch dark; there was not a light on the railway. And just by the wing, where the offices used to be, I suddenly heard a choking cry:

"Mur-der!"

"Who is there?" I called.

Two men were locked in a struggle. One had nearly thrown the other, who was resisting with all his might. And both were breathing heavily.

"Let go!" said one of them and I recognised Ivan Cheprakov. It was he who had cried out in a thin, falsetto voice. "Let go, damn you, or I'll bite your hands!"

The other man I recognised as Moissey. I parted them and could not resist hitting Moissey in the face twice. He fell down, then got up, and I struck him again.

"He tried to kill me," he muttered. "I caught him creeping to his mother's drawer.... I tried to shut him up in the wing for safety."

Cheprakov was drunk and did not recognise me. He stood gasping for breath as though trying to get enough wind to shriek again.

I left them and went back to the house. My wife was lying on the bed, fully dressed. I told her what had happened in the yard and did not keep back the fact that I had struck Moissey.

"Living in the country is horrible," she said. "And what a long night it is!"

"Mur-der!" we heard again, a little later.

"I'll go and part them," I said.

"No. Let them kill each other," she said with an expression of disgust.

She lay staring at the ceiling, listening, and I sat near her, not daring to speak and feeling that it was my fault that screams of "murder" came from the yard and the night was so long.

We were silent and I waited impatiently for the light to peep in at the window. And Masha looked as though she had wakened from a long sleep and was astonished to find herself, so clever, so educated, so refined, cast away in this miserable provincial hole, among a lot of petty, shallow people, and to think that she could have so far forgotten herself as to have been carried away by one of them and to have been his wife for more than half a year. It seemed to me that we were all the same to her—myself, Moissey, Cheprakov; all swept together into the drunken, wild scream of "murder"—myself, our marriage, our work, and the muddy roads of autumn; and when she breathed or stirred to make herself more comfortable I could read in her eyes: "Oh, if the morning would come quicker!"

In the morning she went away.

I stayed at Dubechnia for another three days, waiting for her; then I moved all our things into one room, locked it, and went to town. When I rang the bell at the engineer's, it was evening, and the lamps were alight in Great Gentry Street. Pavel told me that nobody was at home; Victor Ivanich had gone to Petersburg and Maria Victorovna must be at a rehearsal at the Azhoguins'. I remember the excitement with which I went to the Azhoguins', and how my heart thumped and sank within me, as I went up-stairs and stood for a long while on the landing, not daring to enter that temple of the Muses! In the hall, on the table, on the piano, on the stage, there were candles burning; all in threes, for the first performance was fixed for the thirteenth, and the dress rehearsal was on Monday—the unlucky day. A fight against prejudice! All the lovers of dramatic art were assembled; the eldest, the middle, and the youngest Miss Azhoguin were walking about the stage, reading their parts. Radish was standing still in a corner all by himself, with his head against the wall, looking at the stage with adoring eyes, waiting for the beginning of the rehearsal. Everything was just the same!

I went toward my hostess to greet her, when suddenly everybody began to say "Ssh" and to wave their hands to tell me not to make such a noise. There was a silence. The top of the piano was raised, a lady sat down, screwing up her short-sighted eyes at the music, and Masha stood by the piano, dressed up, beautiful, but beautiful in an odd new way, not at all like the Masha who used to come to see me at the mill in the spring. She began to sing:

"Why do I love thee, straight night?"

It was the first time since I had known her that I had heard her sing. She had a fine, rich, powerful voice, and to hear her sing was like eating a ripe, sweet-scented melon. She finished the song and was applauded. She smiled and looked pleased, made play with her eyes, stared at the music, plucked at her dress exactly like a bird which has broken out of its cage and preens its wings at liberty. Her hair was combed back over her ears, and she had a sly defiant expression on her face, as though she wished to challenge us all, or to shout at us, as though we were horses: "Gee up, old things!"

And at that moment she must have looked very like her grandfather, the coachman.

"You here, too?" she asked, giving me her hand. "Did you hear me sing? How did you like it?" And, without waiting for me to answer she went on: "You arrived very opportunely. I'm going to Petersburg for a short time to-night. May I?"

At midnight I took her to the station. She embraced me tenderly, probably out of gratitude, because I did not pester her with useless questions, and she promised to write to me, and I held her hands for a long time and kissed them, finding it hard to keep back my tears, and not saying a word.

And when the train moved, I stood looking at the receding lights, kissed her in my imagination and whispered:

"Masha dear, wonderful Masha!..."

I spent the night at Mikhokhov, at Karpovna's, and in the morning I worked with Radish, upholstering the furniture at a rich merchant's, who had married his daughter to a doctor.

XVII

On Sunday afternoon my sister came to see me and had tea with me.

"I read a great deal now," she said, showing me the books she had got out of the town library on her way. "Thanks to your wife and Vladimir. They awakened my self-consciousness. They saved

134

me and have made me feel that I am a human being. I used not to sleep at night for worrying: 'What a lot of sugar has been wasted during the week.' 'The cucumbers must not be oversalted!' I don't sleep now, but I have quite different thoughts. I am tormented with the thought that half my life has passed so foolishly and half-heartedly. I despise my old life. I am ashamed of it. And I regard my father now as an enemy. Oh, how grateful I am to your wife! And Vladimir. He is such a wonderful man! They opened my eyes."

"It is not good that you can't sleep," I said.

"You think I am ill? Not a bit. Vladimir sounded me and says I am perfectly healthy. But health is not the point. That doesn't matter so much.... Tell me, am I right?"

She needed moral support. That was obvious. Masha had gone, Doctor Blagovo was in Petersburg, and there was no one except myself in the town, who could tell her that she was right. She fixed her eyes on me, trying to read my inmost thoughts, and if I were sad in her presence, she always took it upon herself and was depressed. I had to be continually on my guard, and when she asked me if she was right, I hastened to assure her that she was right and that I had a profound respect for her.

"You know, they have given me a part at the Azhoguins'," she went on. "I wanted to act. I want to live. I want to drink deep of life; I have no talent whatever, and my part is only ten lines, but it is immeasurably finer and nobler than pouring out tea five times a day and watching to see that the cook does not eat the sugar left over. And most of all I want to let father see that I too can protest."

After tea she lay down on my bed and stayed there for some time, with her eyes closed, and her face very pale.

"Just weakness!" she said, as she got up. "Vladimir said all town girls and women are anæmic from lack of work. What a clever man Vladimir is! He is right; wonderfully right! We do need work!"

Two days later she came to rehearsal at the Azhoguins' with her part in her hand. She was in black, with a garnet necklace, and a brooch that looked at a distance like a pasty, and she had enormous earrings, in each of which sparkled a diamond. I felt uneasy when I saw her; I was shocked by her lack of taste. The others noticed too that she was unsuitably dressed and that her earrings and diamonds were out of place. I saw their smiles and heard some one say jokingly:

"Cleopatra of Egypt!"

She was trying to be fashionable, and easy, and assured, and she seemed affected and odd. She lost her simplicity and her charm.

"I just told father that I was going to a rehearsal," she began, coming up to me, "and he shouted that he would take his blessing from me, and he nearly struck me. Fancy," she added, glancing at her part, "I don't know my part. I'm sure to make a mistake. Well, the die is cast," she said excitedly; "the die is cast."

She felt that all the people were looking at her and were all amazed at the important step she had taken and that they were all expecting something remarkable from her, and it was impossible to convince her that nobody took any notice of such small uninteresting persons as she and I.

She had nothing to do until the third act, and her part, a guest, a country gossip, consisted only in standing by the door, as if she were overhearing something, and then speaking a short monologue. For at least an hour and a half before her cue, while the others were walking, reading, having tea, quarrelling, she never left me and kept on mumbling her part, and dropping her written copy, imagining that everybody was looking at her, and waiting for her to come on, and she patted her hair with a trembling hand and said:

"I'm sure to make a mistake.... You don't know how awful I feel! I am as terrified as if I were going to the scaffold."

At last her cue came.

"Cleopatra Alexeyevna—your cue!" said the manager.

She walked on to the middle of the stage with an expression of terror on her face; she looked ugly and stiff, and for half a minute was speechless, perfectly motionless, except for her large earrings which wabbled on either side of her face.

"You can read your part, the first time," said some one.

I could see that she was trembling so that she could neither speak nor open her part, and that she had entirely forgotten the words and I had just made up my mind to go up and say something to her when she suddenly dropped down on her knees in the middle of the stage and sobbed loudly.

There was a general stir and uproar. And I stood quite still by the wings, shocked by what had happened, not understanding at all, not knowing what to do. I saw them lift her up and lead her away. I saw Aniuta Blagovo come up to me. I had not seen her in the hall before and she seemed to have sprung up from the floor. She was wearing a hat and veil, and as usual looked as if she had only dropped in for a minute.

"I told her not to try to act," she said angrily, biting out each word, with her cheeks blushing. "It is folly! You ought to have stopped her!"

Mrs. Azhoguin came up in a short jacket with short sleeves. She had tobacco ash on her thin, flat bosom.

"My dear, it is too awful!" she said, wringing her hands, and as usual, staring into my face. "It is too awful!... Your sister is in a condition.... She is going to have a baby! You must take her away at once...."

In her agitation she breathed heavily. And behind her, stood her three daughters, all thin and flat-chested like herself, and all huddled together in their dismay. They were frightened, over-whelmed just as if a convict had been caught in the house. What a shame! How awful! And this was the family that had been fighting the prejudices and superstitions of mankind all their lives; evidently they thought that all the prejudices and superstitions of mankind were to be found in burning three candles and in the number thirteen, or the unlucky day—Monday.

"I must request ... request ..." Mrs. Azhoguin kept on saying, compressing her lips and accentuating the quest. "I must request you to take her away."

XVIII

A little later my sister and I were walking along the street. I covered her with the skirt of my overcoat; we hurried along through by-streets, where there were no lamps, avoiding the passers-by, and it was like a flight. She did not weep any more, but stared at me with dry eyes. It was about twenty minutes' walk to Mikhok-hov, whither I was taking her, and in that short time we went over the whole of our lives, and talked over everything, and considered the position and pondered....

We decided that we could not stay in the town, and that when I could get some money, we would go to some other place. In some of the houses the people were asleep already, and in others they were playing cards; we hated those houses, were afraid of them, and we talked of the fanaticism, callousness, and nullity of these respectable families, these lovers of dramatic art whom we had frightened so much, and I wondered how those stupid, cruel, slothful, dishonest people were better than the drunken and superstitious peasants of Kurilovka, or how they were better than animals, which also lose their heads when some accident breaks the monotony of their lives, which are limited by their instincts. What would happen to my sister if she stayed at home? What moral torture would she have to undergo, talking to my father and meeting acquaintances every day? I imagined it all and there came into my memory people I had known who had been gradually dropped by their friends and relations, and I remember the tortured dogs which had gone mad, and sparrows plucked alive and thrown into the water—and a whole long series of dull, protracted sufferings which I had seen going on in the town since my childhood; and I could not conceive what the sixty thousand inhabitants lived for, why they read the Bible, why they prayed, why they skimmed books and magazines. What good was all that had been written and said, if they were in the same spiritual darkness and had the same hatred of freedom, as if they were living hundreds and hundreds of years ago? The builder spends his time putting up houses all over the town, and yet would go down to his grave saying "galdary" for "gallery." And the sixty thousand inhabitants had read and heard of truth and mercy and freedom for generations, but to the bitter end they would go on lying from morning to night, tormenting one another, fearing and hating freedom as a deadly enemy.

"And so, my fate is decided," said my sister when we reached home. "After what has happened I can never go there again. My God, how good it is! I feel at peace."

She lay down at once. Tears shone on her eyelashes, but her expression was happy. She slept soundly and softly, and it was clear that her heart was easy and that she was at rest. For a long, long time she had not slept so well.

So we began to live together. She was always singing and said she felt very well, and I took back the books we had borrowed from the library unread, because she gave up reading; she only wanted to dream and to talk of the future. She would hum as she mended my clothes or helped Karpovna with the cooking, or talk of her Vladimir, of his mind, and his goodness, and his fine manners, and his extraordinary learning. And I agreed with her, though I no longer liked the doctor. She wanted to work, to be independent, and to live by herself, and she said she would become a school-teacher or a nurse as soon as her health allowed, and she would scrub the floors and do her own washing. She loved her unborn baby passionately, and she knew already the colour of his eyes and the shape of his hands and how he laughed. She liked to talk of his upbringing, and since the best man on earth was Vladimir, all her ideas were reduced to making the boy as charming as his father. There was no end to her chatter, and everything she talked about filled her with a lively joy. Sometimes I, too, rejoiced, though I knew not why.

She must have infected me with her dreaminess, for I, too, read nothing and just dreamed. In the evenings, in spite of being tired, I used to pace up and down the room with my hands in my pockets, talking about Masha.

"When do you think she will return?" I used to ask my sister. "I think she'll be back at Christmas. Not later. What is she doing there?"

"If she doesn't write to you, it means she must be coming soon."

"True," I would agree, though I knew very well that there was nothing to make Masha return to our town.

I missed her very much, but I could not help deceiving myself and wanted others to deceive me. My sister was longing for her doctor, I for Masha, and we both laughed and talked and never saw that we were keeping Karpovna from sleeping. She would lie on the stove and murmur:

"The samovar tinkled this morning. Tink-led! That bodes nobody any good, my merry friends!"

Nobody came to the house except the postman who brought my sister letters from the doctor, and Prokofyi, who used to come in sometimes in the evening and glance secretly at my sister, and then go into the kitchen and say:

"Every class has its ways, and if you're too proud to understand that, the worse for you in this vale of tears."

He loved the expression—vale of tears. And—about Christmas time—when I was going through the market, he called me into his shop, and without giving me his hand, declared that he had some important business to discuss. He was red in the face with the frost and with vodka; near him by the counter stood Nicolka of the murderous face, holding a bloody knife in his hand.

"I want to be blunt with you," began Prokofyi. "This business must not happen because, as you know, people will neither forgive you nor us for such a vale of tears. Mother, of course, is too dutiful to say anything unpleasant to you herself, and tell you that your sister must go somewhere else because of her condition, but I don't want it either, because I do not approve of her behaviour."

I understood and left the shop. That very day my sister and I went to Radish's. We had no money for a cab, so we went on foot; I carried a bundle with all our belongings on my back, my sister had nothing in her hands, and she was breathless and kept coughing and asking if we would soon be there.

XIX

At last there came a letter from Masha.

"My dear, kind M. A.," she wrote, "my brave, sweet angel, as the old painter calls you, good-bye. I am going to America with my father for the exhibition. In a few days I shall be on the ocean—so far from Dubechnia. It is awful to think of! It is vast and open like the sky and I long for it and freedom. I rejoice and dance about and you see how incoherent my letter is. My dear Misail, give me my freedom. Quick, tear the thread which still holds and binds us. My meeting and knowing you was a ray from heaven, which brightened my existence. But, you know, my becoming your wife was a mistake, and the knowledge of the mistake weighs me down, and I implore you on my knees, my dear, generous friend, quick—quick—before I go over the sea—wire that you will agree to correct our mutual mistake, remove then the only burden on my wings, and my father, who will be responsible for the whole business, has promised me not to overwhelm you with formalities. So, then, I am free of the whole world? Yes?

"Be happy. God bless you. Forgive my wickedness.

"I am alive and well. I am squandering money on all sorts of follies, and every minute I thank God that such a wicked woman as I am has no children. I am singing and I am a success, but it is not a passing whim. No. It is my haven, my convent cell where I go for rest. King David had a ring with an inscription: 'Everything passes.' When one is sad, these words make one cheerful; and when one is cheerful, they make one sad. And I have got a ring with the words written in Hebrew, and this talisman will keep me from losing my heart and head. Or does one need nothing but consciousness of freedom, because, when one is free, one wants nothing, nothing, nothing. Snap the thread then. I embrace you and your sister warmly. Forgive and forget your M."

My sister had one room. Radish, who had been ill and was recovering, was in the other. Just as I received this letter, my sister went into the painter's room and sat by his side and began to read to him. She read Ostrovsky or Gogol to him every day, and he used to listen, staring straight in front of him, never laughing, shaking his head, and every now and then muttering to himself:

"Anything may happen! Anything may happen!"

If there was anything ugly in what she read, he would say vehemently, pointing to the book:

"There it is! Lies! That's what lies do!"

Stories used to attract him by their contents as well as by their moral and their skilfully complicated plot, and he used to marvel at him, though he never called him by his name.

"How well he has managed it."

Now my sister read a page quickly and then stopped, because her breath failed her. Radish held her hand, and moving his dry lips he said in a hoarse, hardly audible voice:

"The soul of the righteous is white and smooth as chalk; and the soul of the sinner is as a pumice-stone. The soul of the righteous is clear oil, and the soul of the sinner is coal-tar. We must work and sorrow and pity," he went on. "And if a man does not work and sorrow he will not enter the kingdom of heaven. Woe, woe to the well fed, woe to the strong, woe to the rich, woe to the usurers! They will not see the kingdom of heaven. Grubs eat grass, rust eats iron...."

"And lies devour the soul," said my sister, laughing.

I read the letter once more. At that moment the soldier came into the kitchen who had brought in twice a week, without saying from whom, tea, French bread, and pigeons, all smelling of scent. I had no work and used to sit at home for days together, and probably the person who sent us the bread knew that we were in want.

I heard my sister talking to the soldier and laughing merrily. Then she lay down and ate some bread and said to me:

"When you wanted to get away from the office and become a house-painter, Aniuta Blagovo and I knew from the very beginning that you were right, but we were afraid to say so. Tell me what power is it that keeps us from saying what we feel? There's Aniuta Blagovo. She loves you, adores you, and she knows that you are right. She loves me, too, like a sister, and she knows that I am right, and in her heart she envies me, but some power prevents her coming to see us. She avoids us. She is afraid."

My sister folded her hands across her bosom and said rapturously:

"If you only knew how she loves you! She confessed it to me and to no one else, very hesitatingly, in the dark. She used to take me out into the garden, into the dark, and begin to tell me in a whisper how dear you were to her. You will see that she will never marry because she loves you. Are you sorry for her?"

"Yes."

"It was she sent the bread. She is funny. Why should she hide herself? I used to be silly and stupid, but I left all that and I am not afraid of any one, and I think and say aloud what I like—and I am happy. When I lived at home I had no notion of happiness, and now I would not change places with a queen."

Doctor Blagovo came. He had got his diploma and was now living in the town, at his father's, taking a rest. After which he said he would go back to Petersburg. He wanted to devote himself to vaccination against typhus, and, I believe, cholera; he wanted to go abroad to increase his knowledge and then to become a University professor. He had already left the army and wore serge clothes, with well-cut coats, wide trousers, and expensive ties. My sister was enraptured with his pins and studs and his red-silk handkerchief, which, out of swagger, he wore in his outside breast-pocket. Once, when we had nothing to do, she and I fell to counting up his suits and came to the conclusion that he must have at least ten. It was clear that he still loved my sister, but never once, even in joke, did he talk of taking her to Petersburg or abroad with him, and I could not imagine what would happen to her if she lived, or what was to become of her child. But she was happy in her dreams and would not think seriously of the future. She said he could go wherever he liked and even cast her aside, if only he were happy himself, and what had been was enough for her.

Usually when he came to see us he would sound her very carefully, and ask her to drink some milk with some medicine in it. He did so now. He sounded her and made her drink a glass of milk, and the room began to smell of creosote.

"That's a good girl," he said, taking the glass from her. "You must not talk much, and you have been chattering like a magpie lately. Please, be quiet."

She began to laugh and he came into Radish's room, where I was sitting, and tapped me affectionately on the shoulder.

"Well, old man, how are you?" he asked, bending over the patient.

"Sir," said Radish, only just moving his lips. "Sir, I make so bold.... We are all in the hands of God, and we must all die.... Let me tell you the truth, sir.... You will never enter the kingdom of heaven."

And suddenly I lost consciousness and was caught up into a dream: it was winter, at night, and I was standing in the yard of the slaughter-house with Prokofyi by my side, smelling of pepper-brandy; I pulled myself together and rubbed my eyes and then I seemed to be going to the governor's for an explanation. Nothing of the kind ever happened to me, before or after, and I can only explain these strange dreams like memories, by ascribing them to overstrain of the nerves. I lived again through the scene in the slaughter-house and the conversation with the governor, and at the same time I was conscious of its unreality.

When I came to myself I saw that I was not at home, but standing with the doctor by a lamp in the street.

"It is sad, sad," he was saying with tears running down his cheeks. "She is happy and always laughing and full of hope. But, poor darling, her condition is hopeless. Old Radish hates me and keeps trying to make me understand that I have wronged her. In his way he is right, but I have my point of view, too, and I do not repent of what has happened. It is necessary to love. We must all love. That's true, isn't it? Without love there would be no life, and a man who avoids and fears love is not free."

We gradually passed to other subjects. He began to speak of science and his dissertation which had been very well received in Petersburg. He spoke enthusiastically and thought no more of my sister, or of his going, or of myself. Life was carrying him away. She has America and a ring with an inscription, I thought, and he has his medical degree and his scientific career, and my sister and I are left with the past.

When we parted I stood beneath the lamp and read my letter again. And I remembered vividly how she came to me at the mill that spring morning and lay down and covered herself with my fur coat—pretending to be just a peasant woman. And another time—also in the early morning—when we pulled the bow-net out of the water, and the willows on the bank showered great drops of water on us and we laughed....

All was dark in our house in Great Gentry Street. I climbed the fence, and, as I used to do in old days, I went into the kitchen by the back door to get a little lamp. There was nobody in the kitchen. On the stove the samovar was singing merrily, all ready for my father. "Who pours out my father's tea now?" I thought. I took the lamp and went on to the shed and made a bed of old newspapers and lay down. The nails in the wall looked ominous as before and their shadows flickered. It was cold. I thought I saw my sister coming in with my supper, but I remembered at once that she was ill at Radish's, and it seemed strange to me that I should have climbed the fence and be lying in the cold shed. My mind was blurred and filled with fantastic imaginations.

A bell rang; sounds familiar from childhood; first the wire rustled along the wall, and then there was a short, melancholy tinkle in the kitchen. It was my father returning from the club. I got up and went into the kitchen. Akhsinya, the cook, clapped her hands when she saw me and began to cry:

"Oh, my dear," she said in a whisper. "Oh, my dear! My God!"

And in her agitation she began to pluck at her apron. On the window-sill were two large bottles of berries soaking in vodka. I poured out a cup and gulped it down, for I was very thirsty. Akhsinya had just scrubbed the table and the chairs, and the kitchen had the good smell which kitchens always have when the cook is clean and tidy. This smell and the trilling of the cricket used to entice us into the kitchen when we were children, and there we used to be told fairy-tales, and we played at kings and queens....

"And where is Cleopatra?" asked Akhsinya hurriedly, breathlessly. "And where is your hat, sir? And they say your wife has gone to Petersburg."

She had been with us in my mother's time and used to bathe Cleopatra and me in a tub, and we were still children to her, and it was her duty to correct us. In a quarter of an hour or so she laid bare all her thoughts, which she had been storing up in her quiet kitchen all the time I had been away. She said the doctor ought to be made to marry Cleopatra—we would only have to frighten him a bit and make him send in a nicely written application, and then the archbishop would dissolve his first marriage, and it would be a good thing to sell Dubechnia without saying anything to my wife, and to bank the money in my own name; and if my sister and I went on our knees to our father and asked him nicely, then perhaps he would forgive us; and we ought to pray to the Holy Mother to intercede for us....

"Now, sir, go and talk to him," she said, when we heard my father's cough. "Go, speak to him, and beg his pardon. He won't bite your head off."

I went in. My father was sitting at his desk working on the plan of a bungalow with Gothic windows and a stumpy tower like the lookout of a fire-station—an immensely stiff and inartistic design. As I entered the study I stood so that I could not help seeing the plan. I did not know why I had come to my father, but I remember that when I saw his thin face, red neck, and his shadow on the wall, I wanted to throw my arms round him and, as Akhsinya had bid me, to beg his pardon humbly; but the sight of the bungalow with the Gothic windows and the stumpy tower stopped me.

"Good evening," I said.

He glanced at me and at once cast his eyes down on his plan.

"What do you want?" he asked after a while.

"I came to tell you that my sister is very ill. She is dying," I said dully.

"Well?" My father sighed, took off his spectacles and laid them on the table. "As you have sown, so you must reap. I want you to remember how you came to me two years ago, and on this very spot I asked you to give up your delusions, and I reminded you of your honour, your duty, your obligations to your ancestors,

144

whose traditions must be kept sacred. Did you listen to me? You spurned my advice and clung to your wicked opinions; further-more, you dragged your sister into your abominable delusions and brought about her downfall and her shame. Now you are both suffering for it. As you have sown, so you must reap."

He paced up and down the study as he spoke. Probably he thought that I had come to him to admit that I was wrong, and probably he was waiting for me to ask his help for my sister and myself. I was cold, but I shook as though I were in a fever, and I spoke with difficulty in a hoarse voice.

"And I must ask you to remember," I said, "that on this very spot I implored you to try to understand me, to reflect, and to think what we were living for and to what end, and your answer was to talk about my ancestors and my grandfather who wrote verses. Now you are told that your only daughter is in a hopeless condition and you talk of ancestors and traditions!... And you can maintain such frivolity when death is near and you have only five or ten years left to live!"

"Why did you come here?" asked my father sternly, evidently affronted at my reproaching him with frivolity.

"I don't know. I love you. I am more sorry than I can say that we are so far apart. That is why I came. I still love you, but my sister has finally broken with you. She does not forgive you and will never forgive you. Your very name fills her with hatred of her past life."

"And who is to blame?" cried my father. "You, you scoundrel!"

"Yes. Say that I am to blame," I said. "I admit that I am to blame for many things, but why is your life, which you have tried to force on us, so tedious and frigid, and ungracious, why are there no people in any of the houses you have built during the last thir-ty years from whom I could learn how to live and how to avoid such suffering? These houses of yours are infernal dungeons in which mothers and daughters are persecuted, children are tor-tured.... My poor mother! My unhappy sister! One needs to drug oneself with vodka, cards, scandal; cringe, play the hypocrite, and go on year after year designing rotten houses, not to see the horror that lurks in them. Our town has been in existence for hun-dreds of years, and during the whole of that time it has not given the country one useful man—not one! You have strangled in em-bryo everything that was alive and joyous! A town of shopkeep-ers, publicans, clerks, and hypocrites, an aimless, futile town, and not a soul would be the worse if it were suddenly razed to the ground."

"I don't want to hear you, you scoundrel," said my father, taking a ruler from his desk. "You are drunk! You dare come into your father's presence in such a state! I tell you for the last time, and you can tell this to your strumpet of a sister, that you will get nothing from me. I have torn my disobedient children out of my heart, and if they suffer through their disobedience and obstinacy I have no pity for them. You may go back where you came from! God has been pleased to punish me through you. I will humbly bear my punishment and, like Job, I find consolation in suffering and unceasing toil. You shall not cross my threshold until you have mended your ways. I am a just man, and everything I say is practical good sense, and if you had any regard for yourself, you would remember what I have said, and what I am saying now."

I threw up my hands and went out; I do not remember what happened that night or next day.

They say that I went staggering through the street without a hat, singing aloud, with crowds of little boys shouting after me:

"Little Profit! Little Profit!"

XX

If I wanted to order a ring, I would have it inscribed: "Nothing passes." I believe that nothing passes without leaving some trace, and that every little step has some meaning for the present and the future life.

What I lived through was not in vain. My great misfortunes, my patience, moved the hearts of the people of the town and they no longer call me "Little Profit," they no longer laugh at me and throw water over me as I walk through the market. They got used to my being a working man and see nothing strange in my carrying paint-pots and glazing windows; on the contrary, they give me orders, and I am considered a good workman and the best contractor, after Radish, who, though he recovered and still paints the cupolas of the church without scaffolding, is not strong enough to manage the men, and I have taken his place and go about the town touting for orders, and take on and sack the men, and lend money at exorbitant interest. And now that I am a contractor I can understand how it is possible to spend several days hunting through the town for slaters to carry out a trifling order. People are polite to me, and address me respectfully and give me tea in the houses where I work, and send the servant to ask me if I would like dinner. Children and girls often come and watch me with curious, sad eyes.

Once I was working in the governor's garden, painting the sum-

146

mer-house marble. The governor came into the summer-house, and having nothing better to do, began to talk to me, and I reminded him how he had once sent for me to caution me. For a moment he stared at my face, opened his mouth like a round O, waved his hands, and said:

"I don't remember."

I am growing old, taciturn, crotchety, strict; I seldom laugh, and people say I am growing like Radish, and, like him, I bore the men with my aimless moralising.

Maria Victorovna, my late wife, lives abroad, and her father is making a railway somewhere in the Eastern provinces and buying land there. Doctor Blagovo is also abroad. Dubechnia has passed to Mrs. Cheprakov, who bought it from the engineer after haggling him into a twenty-per-cent reduction in the price. Moissey walks about in a bowler hat; he often drives into town in a trap and stops outside the bank. People say he has already bought an estate on a mortgage, and is always inquiring at the bank about Dubechnia, which he also intends to buy. Poor Ivan Cheprakov used to hang about the town, doing nothing and drinking. I tried to give him a job in our business, and for a time he worked with us painting roofs and glazing, and he rather took to it, and, like a regular house-painter, he stole the oil, and asked for tips, and got drunk. But it soon bored him. He got tired of it and went back to Dubechnia, and some time later I was told by the peasants that he had been inciting them to kill Moissey one night and rob Mrs. Cheprakov.

My father has got very old and bent, and just takes a little walk in the evening near his house.

When we had the cholera, Prokofyi cured the shopkeepers with pepper-brandy and tar and took money for it, and as I read in the newspaper, he was flogged for libelling the doctors as he sat in his shop. His boy Nicolka died of cholera. Karpovna is still alive, and still loves and fears her Prokofyi. Whenever she sees me she sadly shakes her head and says with a sigh:

"Poor thing. You are lost!"

On week-days I am busy from early morning till late at night. And on Sundays and holidays I take my little niece (my sister expected a boy, but a girl was born) and go with her to the cemetery, where I stand or sit and look at the grave of my dear one, and tell the child that her mother is lying there.

Sometimes I find Aniuta Blagovo by the grave. We greet each other and stand silently, or we talk of Cleopatra, and the child, and the sadness of this life. Then we leave the cemetery and walk in silence and she lags behind—on purpose, to avoid staying with me. The little girl, joyful, happy, with her eyes half-closed against the brilliant sunlight, laughs and holds out her little hands to her, and we stop and together we fondle the darling child.

And when we reach the town, Aniuta Blagovo, blushing and agitated, says good-bye, and walks on alone, serious and circumspect.... And, to look at her, none of the passers-by could imagine that she had just been walking by my side and even fondling the child.

CPSIA information can be obtained
at www.ICGtesting.com
Printed in the USA
LVHW031545120820
663008LV00014B/2476

9 781641 818247